Douglas B. W. Sladen

A summer Christmas

A sonnet upon the S.S. Ballaarat

Douglas B. W. Sladen

A summer Christmas
A sonnet upon the S.S. Ballaarat

ISBN/EAN: 9783741193897

Manufactured in Europe, USA, Canada, Australia, Japa

Cover: Foto ©Andreas Hilbeck / pixelio.de

Manufactured and distributed by brebook publishing software
(www.brebook.com)

Douglas B. W. Sladen

A summer Christmas

A SUMMER CHRISTMAS

AND

A SONNET UPON THE S.S. "BALLAARAT"

BY

DOUGLAS B. W. SLADEN

AN AUSTRALIAN COLONIST

LATE SCHOLAR OF TRINITY COLLEGE, OXFORD ; B.A. OXFORD ;

B.A. AND LL.B. MELBOURNE

AUTHOR OF " FRITHJOF AND INGEBJORG;" "AUSTRALIAN LYRICS;"

"A POETRY OF EXILES," ETC., ETC.

GRIFFITH, FARRAN, OKEDEN, & WELSH

(SUCCESSORS TO NEWBERY AND HARRIS)

WEST CORNER ST PAUL'S CHURCHYARD, LONDON

NEW YORK:

E. P. DUTTON & Co.,
39 WEST 23RD STREET.

TO THE READER.

"A SUMMER CHRISTMAS" itself, like Hudibras or Dr Syntax, does not pretend to be poetry. It is a novel in rhyme,—a thread to string together a number of detached poems, the composition of which has extended over about ten years. The story has been told in rhyme, because Hudibrastic verse is so good a vehicle for conveying succinct pictures of life—in this instance life upon an Australian station (*i.e.*, sheep-station). The idea of writing a novel in verse upon ordinary social life was suggested to me by Mr Coventry Patmore's delicious "Angel in the House." Several tales have been inserted after the manner of Longfellow's "Tales of the Wayside Inn." Some of them have already been published in magazines; and three of them appeared separately in my first volume, "Frithjof and Ingebjorg." "A Summer Christmas" is a sequel to my poem, "The Squire's Brother,"* two personages, Mr and Mrs Forte, appearing in both.

* "The Squire's Brother" has been published in "Frithjof and Ingebjorg and other Poems," by an Australian Colonist (Kegan Paul, Trench & Co.) and "Australian Lyrics" (Griffith & Farran), from whom a few copies may still be obtained.

I shall be satisfied if I awaken in the English reader some interest in the delightful sport and country life of the famous Western District of Victoria, which I have myself enjoyed so often at the invitation of its hospitable squatters ; but I must warn him that there is a vast difference between the life on stations in Victoria belonging to men of established fortune, and the life of a pioneer squatter in the bush, and that I am speaking of holiday time, not attempting to depict the ordinary routine of station life.

The two Homeric tales and the " Song of Nausicaa " were written after re-reading the bulk of the Iliad and the Odyssey, owing to a fresh craving after them, provoked by a perusal of Dr Schliemann's prefaces ; the tale of Helen being finished at sea off the Eastern coast of Australia. " The Last of the Britons," the earliest composed of the tales, was written soon after leaving Cheltenham College.

The "Sonnet to the s.s. 'Ballaarat'" was written upon our last day on board that fine steamer, a ship of nearly five thousand tons, in which I recently returned from Australia.

DOUGLAS BROOKE WHEELTON SLADEN.

INDEX.

A SUMMER CHRISTMAS.

A STORY IN RHYME.

Dedicated to

MRS GEORGE CAWSTON.

DRAMATIS PERSONÆ.

JOHN COBHAM, *a Professor in the Melbourne University. A Man of Kent.*

CHARLES FORTE (*the Squire's Brother*), *a Queensland Squatter and a Victorian Station-holder.*

HELEN FORTE (*the Nellie of the Squire's Brother*), *his Wife.*

MARY RIDLEY, *Governess to Lil and Margaret Forte.*

} *English born.*

WILLIAM FORTE,
PHILIP FORTE,
ELIZABETH FORTE,
MARGARET FORTE,

} *Children of Mr and Mrs Forte.*

KIT JOHNSTONE, *the daughter of a neighbouring Station-holder. An Amazon.*

IDA LEWIS, *a young Widow from Melbourne.*

MAUD MORRISON, *a Melbourne Belle.*

LAUNCELOT, M.P., *an ex-Minister of the Crown in Victoria, nicknamed " Chesterfield."*

ALBERT HALL, *a Bushman—Phil Forte's partner in a Queensland Run.*

LACHLAN SMITH, *a Barrister in the Supreme Court of Victoria.*

} *Australian born.*

The Scene is laid at Waratah Station, a fictitious Station in the Western District of Victoria, beyond Ballaarat.

A SUMMER CHRISTMAS.

At Waratah one Christmastide
Were sitting by the hall-fire side,
With fire unlit, a company
Gathered for the festivity.
'Twas Christmas-eve, and they were at
A station beyond Rallaarat,
Out on the plains.   The paddocks were
Well cleared of timber, scrub and burr,
And English-grassed, the house no hut
Built of bark slabs or boarded cot
But such a mansion as you see
In passing by the Werribee,
Stone built, with gardens well laid out
In gay beds, planted all about
With choice exotic shrubs and trees
And all that could subserve or please
A wool-king with a broad freehold
All round his home, and flocks untold
On his huge runs on Queensland downs,
And, though far off from seaport towns,
With every luxury, now brought
From home, for wife and children bought.
    Most noticeable of them all

A

Around the fireside in the hall
Was this prince of the squatterhood,
Who, standing in his stockings, stood
Six feet and inches almost three,
Strong, and of hand and speech so free,
And still as active as a lad,
Though sixty years and hardships had
Grizzled his hair and beard with grey;
A hero who had fought his way,
From pittance left him by his sire
(As younger brother of the squire),
To wealth immense by years of toil,
Exiled from whites, and in turmoil
With hostile blacks, out on a run
Far west, beneath a Queensland sun,
He who had once been known at Court
And in the Clubs as "Cupid" Forte.
    No trace of ceremoniousness
Retained he now, though none the less
Was he a graceful well-bred host;
But he was hearty in accost,
And giving the Australian grip
And good up-country fellowship
As bushmen.   Few books had he read,
But good ones, and he truly said
That he had mastered their contents.
He'd sat in early parliaments,
And by his fellows been esteemed,
Though no great speaker, for he seemed
To do his best for everyone,
And always used a courteous tone;

A Summer Christmas.

And when such crises came about
As made men fear to speak, spoke out
With simple sense, what others thought
But how to best dissemble sought.
Close to her husband sat his wife,
Some years his junior in life,
And with her hair scarce changed a whit
Since they were wed.   Yet shades would flit
Across her bright plaits 'neath the sun,
And grey hairs 'mid the gold were none.
E'en yet one noted that she bore
The same slim figure as of yore,
And marked a majesty of gait
Which had been grace at twenty-eight
(The year her lord had crossed the foam
To fetch her to his Austral home),
And that her charms were scarce impaired.
 All of her children had been spared,
And now were round her;—Margaret,
The youngest, well-grown, but not yet
Out of the shy and modest awe
That urges childhood to withdraw
Or hang its head in company.
Dark-haired, with clear dark cheeks was she,
And had beneath her brow such eyes
As chained onlookers with surprise,
So weirdly blue, and spiritual,
And fathomless, were they withal.
 The eldest, Will, was huge of limb
As was his Father, so like him
That, had he worn a bearded chin,

And had his grizzled hair, no twin
Could have been closer. He had pulled
In the great boat race, but had mulled
His " little-go " (for he was bred
At Cambridge), and could with his head
Only remember points of sheep
And racehorse pedigrees, and keep
Note of his thousand kindly friends,
And scraps of business odds and ends.
In college days he was not wild,
But merely boisterous. No child
More simple, or more innocent
Of sin, and guile, and blandishment.
College had not unfitted him
For station life, but it would seem
Had given him fresh interest,
And added, as it were, a zest,
As if for real work his will
Had a great vacuum to fill.
    He rode with fearless skill, and shot
Like a backwoodsman, and feared not
Into a swamp neck-deep to wade
When he a mob of ducks waylaid,
Or crawl on belly through a sedge
Hissing with snakes, to reach its edge.
He was as kind as he was brave,
And with less pleasure took than gave ;
And, though he loved society
And sports, he'd bid them all good-bye,
And work for months upon the runs
In Queensland, not like squatters' sons,

As rich as he was, often do,
But like a bushman staunch and true.
He was beloved alike by men
And women : once within his ken
You could but love his simple soul.
    As far from him as pole from pole
Was Phil (though upright, yet so far
From the pure heart which like a star
Shone through his brother's life), sunk down,
As men of best intents must own
They have, by striking out too deep,
And, being then obliged to keep
Head above water, clutching at
Means they'd have shrunk from but for that.
In person, rather short than tall,
With the blue eyes that marked them all,
And handsomer than Will, and more
Like what his Father 'd been of yore.
He dressed much like an Englishman
Of well-bred fashion, spick and span,
In gloves and hats, and with his coats
Well cut but not extreme, his boots
The best that could be bought. He'd go
To Melbourne oft as a wool show
Or sale of stud sheep gave excuse,
Stay at the Club a month, and use
The hundred opportunities
Showered by fashion's votaries
Upon him (soon as they should chance
To hear that he'd arrived), to dance
And tennis. When he went, he stayed

Beyond good resolutions made
Ere starting ; but still, conscience moved
Him thus far, that, though much he loved
Club life and town, he would not go
Without excuse of sale or show.
  Will was the eldest, next came Phil,
And then Elizabeth, called Lil,
Partly to chime with " Phil " and " Will,"
Partly from the Australian hate
For homely names, like Jane and Kate,
Mary and Sarah.   They delight
To verge upon the opposite,
With Rubys, Hildas, Violets,
Gladyses, Idas, and Jeannettes,
Lorraines, and Pearls, and Isobels,
And Harolds, Kenneths, Lionels.
They'd had a fight that very day,
Ere dinner had been cleared away,
Over this much-vexed theme of names,
The English urging ancient claims
For Mary and its congeners,
The colonists preferring theirs
As nicer and more musical.
And then, some one proposed that all
In order should declare their own.
And first came the Professor's, John,
And then Miss Forte's, her name was Lil,
And therefore was on their part still
Said one side, but Elizabeth
The other.   Next was Lachlan Smith,
A brisk young 'wig' from Temple Court,

A Summer Christmas.

Ready to cut his mother short,
And argue with her on his birth,
Or any other thing on earth,
Or out of it. Next him was Maud,
Maud Morrison, whom men applaud
As one of Melbourne's belles ; next her,
Will Forte; and next a character—
A widow, exquisitely dressed
(And not in widow's weeds), confessed
A sorceress, although she lacked
The charms of person which attract
The passer-by : her Christian name
Was Ida. She the gentle flame
Had lit, 'twas rumoured, in the breast
Of the ex-minister addressed
As Chesterfield (a man with grace
Of action and a pleasing face,
Who sat on Mrs Forte's right hand),
So exquisite was he, and bland
In manner, letter, speech, and smile,
But yet upright and without guile,
Liked upon both sides of the House,
For no attack on him could rouse
His tongue to personalities
Levelled against their enemies
By M.P.'s in Assemblies new ;
A prepossessing man to view.
One liked to meet his figure slim
The more, the more one knew of him.
Some wag, with envy half-concealed,
Had christened him " The Chesterfield

Of Melbourne," and the soubriquet
Had gradually made its way
Into the press, society,
And lastly his own family.
The widow sat upon the right
Of Mr Forte, and opposite
Miss Ridley, the girls' governess
(They were grown up, but kept her less
As teacher than companion), fair,
With smoothly plaited flaxen hair;
A vicar's daughter from the north,
Of a poor race of ancient birth.
Next her was Phil, and next to him,
Full woman, therefore not too slim,
But with a form of slender grace,
And with bright health writ on her face
In rosy cheeks and clear brown skin,
With grey eyes, classic nose and chin,
And curly hair, cut short behind,
Was Kit, a medley, both refined
And fast in instinct, delicate
In taste, but proof to bear her fate
In sports and hardships masculine,
Proud, and with courage leonine,
Full of wit and good fellowship,
And with the curved lines of her lip,
As prone to melt in laughter, born
Of pure fun, as to curl in scorn;
Di. Vernon's rival in the chase,
Queen of the men's hearts in the place
And miles around, but far from love

A Summer Christmas.

And wooing as the moon above,
The chaste, cold planet. She would rove
With horse or gun, the whole day long,
A month with the same lover, strong
In her robust celibacy,
Brimming with grace, her voice and eye
Full of bright mirth and happiness :
But if her frankness made him press
The claims of love, a soft firm voice,
Half laugh, half anger, gave him choice
Of instant change or banishment.
As far as maiden may, she went
As man meets man, and her delight
Was so contagious that one might
Mistake the light of smile and glance
For sign of more significance.

    Dressed for the field, she wore a tweed
Made jacket-fashion, short-skirted,
Revealing all a slim arched foot
Laced in a natty shooting boot,
Replaced at early morn and night
By low-heeled pump of leather bright.

    Full dressed she wore no jewellery,
And went in for simplicity,
With rich plain stuffs, good work and fit.

    Her father's station much of it
Joined Mr Forte's, and rumour said
That Phil, if he'd his way, would wed
His handsome neighbour. A contrast
Was Lil, whose girlhood stood aghast
At Kit's rough sports and manner based

On manly canons of good taste,
Though she rode gracefully and well,
Played tennis fairly, and could tell
Of triumphs too.   She was petite,
With slender waist, and pretty feet
In dainty Paris shoes, and dressed
In stuffs and fashions daintiest.
Her clear skin was of the warm hue
That marks the south, and o'er it grew
In wavy clusters the fair hair
Of Gothic ancestry ; a pair
Of liquid eyes spoke gentleness,
A heart most kindly to distress,
Most tender when besieged by love,
And true to home though it might rove.
Gracefully danced she, lightly swayed,
And tastefully the keys she played,
Whether for Lied of Mendelssohn
Or new waltz she was called upon.
She'd a smooth voice but did not sing,
Most prudently considering
That one more poor executante
Could not be called a social want.

   She 'd not, her lovers must confess,
The noble, queenly loveliness
And rosy health that Kit could boast,
But the soft charms which we accost
Sooner and guard more tenderly,
The suppliant hand, the wistful eye,
The pleading voice, the tender mien ;
Nor had she the robust and keen

Brain of the other, but her mind
Was healthy and enough refined
To glean some joy from books and art,
And the æsthetic tastes which part
The cultured from the common herd.
   On Kit's left sat, without a word,
But with a shrewd wink in his eye, .
Which shewed that, opportunity
Requiring, he his views could state,
If not with fluency, with weight,
A stalwart man, with crisp bleached beard
And sunburnt face, with both hands seared
By scars and stains, and legs much bowed,
As if he far and often rode :
His name was Albert Hall, his seat
Was next to blue-eyed Margaret :
Beyond was Chesterfield, who said
That he was Launcelot : at the head
Sat Helen, handsome Mrs Forte,
Her lord was Charlie.   In the sport
Which followed, parties differed not
On Lachlan, Ida, Launcelot,
Albert and Maud, but each side sought
To reckon Helen and Margaret,
These since in Scottish homes they'd met
Helens and Maggies everywhere,
And those because the names were fair
And fanciful.   Debate ran high
Between the rivals as to why
One chose names in so high a strain,
And one so simple and so plain.

None could convince and none would yield,
So they referred to Chesterfield,
Who appositely answered thus :
   " If you reflect, it's obvious
Why Cobhams, who have lived in Kent
For centuries, should be content,
Age after age, to call a son
By the ancestral name of John.
But why my sire, who did not know
His own grandfather, should do so,
He failed to see, and therefore chose,
As I have reason to suppose,
What doubtless he esteemed to be
The name of names, and christened me
After his favourite Launcelot.
   And so both sides can urge somewhat,
You with the humble name of John
Remembering that you're the son
Of twenty in succession,
Traced with all due minutiæ
Upon a parchment pedigree,
While I, named after Arthur's knight,
Call to my mind the legends bright
About him, caring nought because
I don't know who my grandsire was."
   His answer met with much applause,
But not with Lachlan Smith's—the jest,
At himself aimed by Launcelot, pressed
Harder on him, being the son
Of storekeepers at Flemington,
And striving to conceal his birth,

By all the Lachlans of the earth
Being claimed as his affinities.
Nor did it altogether please
Maud, though she could evince at once,
By claiming all the Morrisons
As kinsfolk, that his satire sly
Did not in her own case apply.
  But Smith was one who well deserved
All his success. He never swerved
From his high purpose, and his rise
Was due entirely to his wise
Exertions and abilities.
A state-school boy, he had obtained
Grammar school scholarships, then gained
A college bursary and high
Distinctions as each year went by
While at the University.
Called to the Bar then, he had made
His way by hard work undismayed.
Too shallow and self-satisfied,
Like many self-raised men untried
With educations of a zone
More cultivated than their own,
He was, but, all things said and done,
Praiseworthy. Contrast could be none
Greater than was between this one
And Cobham, the Oxonian,
In every sense a gentleman,
Man of the world and scholar, tall,
Of lithe build, and symmetrical,
With well-shaped head well set upon

Square shoulders, clean shaved face whereon
Was no hair save the black moustache,
With eyes that seemed to cloud or flash
With ev'ry thought.   His hair was grey,
And had been silvered many a day,
Though he was still young and no care
Or grief had fallen to his share.
He had a certain easy grace
In each expression of his face
And motion of his body, voice
Alluring, power to rejoice
In diverse objects marvellous.
Science, the beauties various
Of Nature, Art, Society
(The pleasure-seeking and the high),
And sports of active exercise,
Fair women and grand enterprise,
All had their charms for him : he'd come
To his professorship from home,
And Chesterfield had taken him
To set him in the social swim,
And these last hospitalities
Were due to his good offices,
And he had come himself to make
The week go well for Cobham's sake.
   'Twas Christmas-eve, and they sat round
Th' hearth filled with wattlebloom still found
On stray trees, and with Christmas-Bush
From New South Wales, and Bottle-Brush,
And snowy spikes of bayonet grass,
And treefern fronds and Sassafras.

After dessert on summer nights,
Those who stayed in to have the lights
For work or reading used the hall,
Being the coolest room of all,
Tiled, and with many openings
And passages to rooms and wings;
But most went out, the men to smoke
In the Verandah, women folk
To hear the words of wisdom come
From them in intervals of fume.
   However, being Christmas-eve
They all were in the hall, to give
The night its due, with raisins snapped
Out of the burning brandy, capped
With dance and bumper of champagne.
But first they talked in idle strain,
And lounged about as people do
An after dinner hour or two,
And sat down, one by one, around
Where in the winter warmth was found,
And all with empty hands, save one
Who skimmed through the Decameron.
"What's the book, Chesterfield?" cried Will.
" Boccaccio," he said.   Then Lil,
"Who or what was Boccaccio?"
Whom the Professor answered, " Know
That some five hundred years ago
To northern Italy there came
A deadly pestilence, the same
As England christened the Black Death,
And to escape its mortal breath

From Florence fled three noblemen,
And seven ladies fair.   The ten
Beguiled the tedium of their stay
By choosing from themselves each day
A king or queen of sports ; each told
Each day a story new or old
Worth telling, till ten days were o'er,
And then to Florence turned once more."
"Famous," cried Lil, " why should not we
Have a Decameron?   But you see,"
She added, " There are fourteen here
And eight days: that would interfere
With having kings and queens : and I
And Madge—why, half the family
Could not tell tales."   Said Chesterfield,
To whom they for advice appealed,
" We could not—all of you must own—
Well stomach a Decameron,
But I have a proposal . . ."   Each
Cried " Listen," while he made his speech.
He said, " To tell ten tales a day
Would take our time too much away,
And half of us would be too shy
Their skill in telling tales to try,
And some might fail : so I suggest
That the professor should be pressed
To be the spokesman every night,
And we draw lots to have the right
To choose the subject—none choose twice."
And all agreed to his advice.
And as for dance or snapdragon

Or toasts 'twas early yet, some one
Begged that he should begin at once,
And drew to see who for the nonce
Should be the King or Queen.   It fell
To Mrs Forte, who bade him tell
Of fair wife loving husband well.
Then he, " It seems that my consent
Has been presumed : but while content
To do your will, I claim your grace
Where'er my tale exhibits trace
Of inconsistency in work,
Being extempore.   The Turk,
Or rather Arab, by your leave
My subject of to-night shall give.

SAIDA, THE BELOVED OF THE CALIPH.

Haroun Al Raschid, it is said,
Was in his palace at Baghdad,
Sitting one summer day at noon,
And ready with the heat to swoon ;
When in the dusty shadeless square
He spied an Arab drawing near,
Jaded, and limping sore, and wan.
And when the Caliph looked thereon,
And saw him toiling up the road,
He cried out, " Hath Almighty God,
Ever since heaven and earth began,
Made such a wholly wretched man
As this who drags his blistered feet

B

At such an hour up the scorched street ?"
And, turning to the vizier,
He bade that if the traveller
Craved audience with him that day,
He should be brought to him straightway.
And so it fell out as he thought,
And the poor man to him was brought,
And, supplicating much, began
To make complaint against Merwan—
Who, at Medina's holy gate,
Gave justice for the Caliphate.

"Commander of the Faithful, I —
Now eaten by calamity—
Was once of all men happiest,
With a fair wife and loving blest,
And a young camel trained, whereby
Our food and raiment to supply :
But one by one misfortunes came,
And false friends fell of, as the flame
Dies when the substance of the wood
Is into empty ash subdued ;
And last of all came my wife's sire,
And, with well simulated ire,
Snatched my last treasure from me too.
And so I took my staff, and drew
To Merwan, our lord Governor,
And made complaint with groanings sore :

Who at the first lent ready ear,
And bade mine enemy appear ;
Who, when he came, with lying word,
Cried that of her own free accord
She had left me and sought her home,
And that when, after I had come
To crave her to return to me,
She had entreated him that he
Would not allow her to be led
Back to the loathsomeness she fled.
So that I, fearing that his tale
Would with the Governor prevail,
Asked whether, if my wife were brought
Before him, and herself besought
To be restored to me once more,
He would compel them to restore :
Who answered that it should be so,
And bade mine adversary go
And bring the woman to his seat,
That he might judge her as was meet —
Who, coming back, with him did bring
My wife, shamefaced and quivering.
And she, when bidden to declare
Which of us two the truth did swear,
Spake up for me in such a wise
That Merwan—fain with his own eyes
To see the woman, who could say
That which he would in such a way—

Bade her uncover in that place,
And show the fashon of her face.
And she did so with shame and wince,
And he—whereas a minute since
He had adjudged her mine—perforce
Now made me crave him for divorce,
And took my wife to be his bride.
And therefore, weary and red-eyed,
In the mid-heat of a noonday
I drag my swollen feet, to lay
Suit for redress at thy divan,
And justice on the lord Merwan."

Nor did he sue without avail—
For when the Caliph heard his tale
Dark grew his eyeballs, and he sent
Letters of passionate intent
That bade Merwan give back the wife,
If he set any worth on life,
Or, by the Prophet's holy beard,
And by the sepulchre revered,
His headless body should be meat
For dogs and vultures in the street.

Then Merwan, as the Caliph bade,
Did send the woman to Baghdad.
And sent before her couriers,
Bearing such words as these, in verse : —

" Commander of the Faithful, I
Bend low to thine authority.
This Arab came to me to crave
Justice: and ready ear I gave,
As might beseem the judge who stands
To execute thy just commands.
He said that when prosperity
Had run ahead and passed him by,
The father of his wife had come
And haled her back to her old home,
And kept her there in his despite,
And prayed that I would do him right. .
I, willing to do what was meet,
Called forthwith to the judgment seat
The wrong-doer, who, when he came,
And heard the count, denied the same,
Asserting that his child had fled
For succour, and yet lived in dread
Of being forced to dwell again
With the most hateful of all men.

Whereat the suppliant craved that I
Would have her brought to make reply,
And if so 'twere that she, when brought, .
To be restored to him, besought,
That I would bid her sire restore
The woman unto him once more.

And they returned in no long time
With one who seemed in the young prime
Of comely graceful womanhood,
Out of whose close-drawn veil there glowed
Two eyes that shot a mingled flame
Of sorrow, love, surprise and shame;
Who, when I bade her to declare
Which of the twain the truth did swear,
Spake for her lord in such a wise
That I was fain with mine own eyes
To see the fashioning of face
And somewhat further of the grace
Of this wise woman, who could say
That which she would in such a way,
And bade her draw her veil aside:
Whereat with shame the ruddy tide
Filled all the fairness of her cheeks,
And mid the shamefacedness that speaks
Of gentleness and modesty,
With trembling touch, she did comply,
And stood before my greedy eyes
A houri out of paradise,
Unmatched for soft alluring grace.
My heart leapt from me in that place
To touch the lips that could confess
With such sweet wisdom her distress,
And to be lord of her whose love
Misfortunes only helped to prove,

And with persuasion did enforce
Her husband to obtain divorce,
And had the woman to my heart,
The which she took in loving part
Until thy firman came to me.
Her to this end I send to thee,
That thou may'st look on her and know
What gifts hath Allah to bestow
On woman if he mindeth to.
Nor do I think that, when thine eyes
Have looked on her, thou wilt despise
Thy servant for what he hath done,
But that thou'lt take her for thine own
Unto the grand Seraglio
Whereby the Tigris' waters flow."

Whereat the Caliph chafed again,
And cried, "This shameless one of men
Shall die the death who first deprives
My faithful Arabs of their wives,
And afterward accuseth me,
Saying that I have but to see
Her who hath brought about his blame
And that my sin will be the same;"
Then, turning to his vizier, bade
Bring forward him who sought his aid,
And said, "Thy wife to-day hath come,
And thou shalt have her to thine home;

But stay thou until first I see
What manner of woman this may be
Who speaketh with such honied lips,
And whose eyes' magic doth eclipse
The magic of all eyes in glance,
Of which Merwan hath cognizance.
And then do thou and she depart
Whereso on earth it likes thy heart."

Now she, for all her late resort
With Merwan at Medina's court,
Was as shamefaced and full of dread
When to the Caliph she was led,
And bidden to unveil her head,
As she had been when she was brought
To Merwan's palace and besought;
And, when before the throne, she stood
In all her peerless womanhood,
As beautiful as Ayesha,
Upon whose fragrant bosom lay
The prophet's cheek in happy hours,
And whose fair hands, like lily flowers,
Were wreathed about his dying head,
Or Zeineb who was wife of Zeid,
Or Mary the Egyptian,
While down her face a tear there ran,
As pure as Zemzem's sacred spring,
From eyes, like dog's eyes, questioning

What was the feeling and intent
Of those whose gaze on her was bent
Whether it boded good or ill.

Meanwhile the Caliph drank his fill
Of this love-potion, and did muse
If he might not e'en now refuse
The boon he gave a moment since,
And yet do nothing that a prince
Who loved his people might not do.
And seemed it that, if it were so
That he might win the man's consent
With princely presents well content,
There should be little harm though he
Kept back the houri-eyed to be
A crown of loving to his life.

Natheless the Arab loved his wife
So graciously that for her sake,
Though beggared, he was loath to take
Three virgins, fair as the full moon,
And each of them as portion
Having a thousand gold dinars,
And for himself in the bazaars
To have all men bow low to him,
With downcast eyes and bended limb,
Like a great officer of state,
And to take from the Caliphate

Much gold and raiment by the year,
But answer made with many a tear,

"Caliph of Islam, I indeed
Came to thee in my utmost need
To claim thy hand's protection
Against the arm of Hakam's son :
But lo, thy little finger is
Thicker than Merwan's loin, I wis,
Nor do I know to whom to turn
For aid against thy purpose stern.
Take back thy gifts—I heed them not,
Though poor and painful be my lot ;
I would not change my low estate
To have the very Caliphate,
If to have it were to lose her." ·
The Caliph said, " Thou didst aver
That thou hadst put her from thy breast,
And Merwan's letter hath confessed
That he hath also done likewise.
How was she pleasing in thine eyes
Whom thou didst put away from thee ?
Now shall she choose between us three,
Thyself, and Hakam's son, and me :
If she choose thee, she shall be thine,
And, if she choose thee not, be mine.
Dost thou agree ? "

                The Arab bowed,

And straight the Caliph cried aloud,
" Say, Saida, whether wilt thou wed
The Sheik of Islam to thy bed,
Who sits upon the Prophet's seat,
With all the nations at his feet,
And dwells in golden palaces,
And hath great realms and satrapies,
And slaves, and riches, and empire,
And can give all thou canst desire ?
Or wilt thou have the lord Merwan,
That tyrannous and wrongful man,
Who loveth thee so well, forsooth,
That the poor lover of thy youth,
Was driven, and constrained, perforce,
To sue unto him for divorce ?
Or wilt thou have this wretched one,
Who hath not to his portion,
Save hunger and, her mother, need ? "
" By Allah," she replied, " indeed,
Caliph of Islam, know that I
Do not desert when night is nigh
Those, whom I love in the broad day,
Because the sunshine sinks away ;
Nor do I change as the times do,
And, when the summer flies, fly too ;
Nor can I easily forget
That I have been his amulet
And ewe-lamb, from the very first ;

Nor are our old love-bonds yet burst,
That have grown like an ivy stem,
As year by year passed over them.
O Sir, should I not bear with him,
Now that the nights are wild and dim,
Who have with him lived cloudless days,
When he basked in the spring sun's rays.
It is the common way of men,
Like deer who dwell upon the plain,
While the sun shines, and peace is there,
To browse together free from care,
But when the wolves come with the night
To forget all things in their fright,
And each cry, "Save himself who can."
As with the deer, so with the man.
But woman is not ever so ;
Her love shines with as pure a glow
Right through the darkness, mist, and spray,
As the North star which guides the way
Of mariners on unknown seas.

"O Caliph, I am such as these,
And rather had I starve and die
With yon poor Arab, miserably,
Than share the grandeur of thy court,
Or with the base Merwan consort."

Haroun saluted as Al Raschid,

Caliph of Islam, the Abbassid,
Who sate upon the Prophet's seat,
And had the nations at his feet,
And dwelt in golden palaces,
Had seldom such reply as this,
And greatly doubted if his ear
Retained the faculty to hear,
But to his royal word adhered
And swore that, by the Prophet's beard,
Even so he would, and more also,
Unto the son of Hakam do
If ever afterward he pressed
This Saida from her Arab's breast,
And gave him charge to use his power
For their well-faring from that hour.
The Caliph Haroun Al Raschid
Many a deed of bloodshed did,
And many evil works wrought he;
But this good shall remembered be
How that he kept his royal word
In giving Saida to her lord.

He ceased: and when th' applause was hushed
Which hailed his effort, somewhat flushed
At having stepped into the breach
With even this small maiden speech,
" Thank you, Professor," Helen said,
" For the grand way in which you've pled

For women.   If we have one claim
Unquestioned to heroic fame,
It is that we pause not to test
Whether our idol be the best
Of gold, or merely common clay,
And scorn with scales its worth to weigh.
Your shaft struck where you took not aim,
For ere to this bright land I came
I was betrothed for ten whole years
Of trials, disappointments, fears
And . . ."   " Now wife no tales out of school !"
" And I was laughed at for a fool
For holding true so many a day
To one twelve thousand miles away.
And you, with your pretended frowns,
Were, on the day you left the Downs,
No great catch for a girl who weighed
The value of the match she made ;
And I had suitors in my youth,
Instance your brother, who in truth
Were much to be preferred to you,
By one who took the worldly view.
For you were but a younger son,
Starting to try a backblock run
In Queensland, but (don't frown at me)
I always fancied you to be
A higher being, quite above
All human standards except love."

     *   *   *   *

When she had finished her romance
Will pushed the chairs back for a dance,

And Mrs Forte sat down and played
Waltz after waltz, in long cascade,
With the well-modulated touch
Of one who had herself danced much.
All danced but Mr Forte, and Kit
Who would not dance, esteeming it
Effeminate for one who tried
To break the social fetters, tied
Round the weak hands of maid and wife,
And share the liberty and life
Which men usurp : and this though she
Could, when she chose, dance faultlessly
With the proud pose and noble air
So enviable and so rare.
  Waltz after waltz Maud danced with Phil,
Because the Oxford man and Will,
Although they both danced fairly well,
In the last step did not excel,
And Chesterfield could only do
The deux-temps.   Lachlan Smith, 'twas true,
Could dance the new step, but then he
In ease and poise failed woefully,
Although he pleased himself : and Hall
Could not be said to dance at all,
Although he briskly twisted round
His victims, whom he mostly found
In bashful, blue-eyed Margaret
(Who had not very often yet
Tried in society the steps
She did so well with Meinherr Kreps,
Who trained most Melbourne ladies' schools

In dancing and deportment's rules),
And Mary Ridley, who had come
From a strict-low-church vicar's home,
Where dancing was esteemed a sin,
And stimulant as bad as gin.
Kind-hearted Will danced turn about
With Madge, who, having not come out,
And being shy and scarce full grown,
Might have been too much left alone,
And with his sisters' governess,
As chosen by the others less,
And Ida Lewis, who could dance
Only deux-temps (*the* step in France
When she was there at school, she said,
Which, if she spoke correctly, made
Her sweet and thirty).   Lastly, Lil
Won praise from even captious Phil,
So perfect in her steps was she,
In pose so upright and so free,
And yet so yielding and so light.
    Maud Morrison perhaps was quite
Her equal in mere stepping skill,
But lacked the gentle grace of Lil.
With Maud first the Professor danced,
Who was not much thereby advanced
In his good graces : she in fact
Repelled him with a want of tact.
The next he danced with Margaret,
Who started the new step, but yet
Adapted her step easily
To his, when she perceived that he

Preferred the trois temps, though to all
His efforts conversational
On twenty topics she replied
Laconically : then he tried
Miss Ridley, who displayed no ease
And little grace, and by degrees
Fell out of step ; and then he walked
To where Kit Johnstone stood and talked
For half-an-hour, revelling
In her bright chat, and noticing
The shades of humour which gave chase
One to another o'er her face.
He did not dare ask Lil to dance,
Though he stole many a longing glance,
As round and round she floated by
On her light feet so gracefully
In the new step,—Maud Morrison
Had been so galling in her tone,
Because he danced trois temps, and she
Danced not her steps so daintily
As Lil : and so he stood with Kit,
Half satisfied with her arch wit,
Half taking his faint heart to task
That what he wished he dared not ask.
But as they talked Lil came and cried,
" Professor, dance with me, you've tried,
With all the others. I can do
Your step, for I was watching you
When you were with Maud Morrison,
And if I fail, why no harm's done."
And then they started, and he thought

That he till then had never caught
The perfect luxury and grace
Of waltzing : so exact each pace
Fell into unison with his,
So full of subtle witcheries
Was the light form within his grasp,
So hearty-innocent the clasp
Of the small thrilling fingers thrust
Within his in such perfect trust.
And when at last the music ceased,
She thanked him with a smile as pleased
As if the honours of it lay
With him, not her, then led the way
To a broad lounge which stood before
The opening of the boudoir door,
Inside, and, making room for him,
Crossed on a stool her ankles slim,
And, leaning back, talked softly on,
How she'd enjoyed the dance just done,
And begged him once again to tell
The tale he'd lately told so well.
  'Twas rather Lily's way to form
Quite suddenly attachments warm,
And, when she did so, all her grace
And tenderness and pretty face
Were requisitioned to advance
Development of her romance.
She was so lovingly inclined,
And so romantic in her mind,
That she had aye some idol shrined
And pedestalled within her heart,

And, when with one compelled to part,
Was hungry-souled and ill at rest
Till she was once again possessed :
Thus fiercely her hot southern blood
Strove with the cold of maidenhood.
　　She was a very child of love,
So marvellously could she move,
With glance and finger, thrill and voice,
All men, who met her, to rejoice.
She looked so full back to their eyes,
She clasped their hand in such a wise,
Her tones were pitched so sweet and low
That all she told them seemed as though
There were some special confidence.
And yet 'twas all in innocence
And worship.　The professor came
Just in the nick of time : the flame
Of the last love was hardly quenched,
And no new fetters had been clenched,
And he precisely was the man
Most likely to create and fan
The ' sacred fire ' within her breast,
Being at once the cleverest
And one of the best-looking men
Who'd ever come into her ken.
He dressed well, talked well, played at games
Well enough to support his claims
With most chance rivals, had a name
For books and scholarship, and came
Of ancient lineage.　She fell
Into this new magician's spell

As soon as she had heard him tell
The legend about Saida,
So tenderly did he pourtray
A loving woman's constancy
And modest girl's timidity,
That seemed it that who thus could tell
Of woman's heart must know it well,
And set her longing to find out
What tenderness there was about
His own heart.   Thus these two sat on,
And she asked many a question
About this Saida.   But he
Knew nothing of her history,
Save that he'd read in volumes old
The outline of the tale he told.
  She asked him if he cared again
To dance, and in condoling strain
Listened to the delinquencies
Of scornful Maud, and said that his
Was one of the most pleasant steps
She ever danced to, that Herr Kreps
Had said the " trois temps " was the best
Of all waltz steps—and all the rest
Which sympathetic girls do say
When they are carried right away
With championing some pet cause,
As ardent Lily just then was.

*   *   *   *

Their confidences were cut short
By a stern summons to the sport
Of snapping dragons from a dish,

With blazing brandy devilish,
Followed by bumpers of champagne
To welcome Christmas back again.
And ere they parted, after they
Had wished a Merry Christmas-day
And many of them, each to each,
The kind host made a short neat speech :
" Welcome to Waratah, young men,
Look to the ladies first, and then
Do all that in your pow'r you can
To show our guest, the Englishman,
The pleasures with which station-life
Can be in holidays made rife.
He entertains us every night,
So it is only fair and right
That we should show him all we may
Of our life and its joys by day."

Christmas Day, December 25th.

Waratah breakfasts were at nine :
Lil was down first and looked divine
In a fresh, simple, morning dress
Of gossamer, with snowiness
Unbroken save by sash pale blue
Wound round her, and a spray or two
Of the wild brook forget-me-not
Pinned in a cluster at her throat.
The others followed.   One could see
Who were for church quite easily
Without appealing to the vote.
Old Mr Forte in his frock coat
And Chesterfield looked most devout :
Maud Morrison was much decked out,
And Mrs Forte wore rich black silk,
Margaret ' Surah,' white as milk,
Miss Ridley her best summer white,
While the Professor came down dight
In Paget suit of iron-grey twill
And stiff white waistcoat.   Only Lil
Was neutral.   Kit was careless in
A Norfolk jacket masculine,
And Phil and Will wore old tweed clothes,
Which told as plainly as would oaths
How much church service they would hear,
And Hall replied with prompt " No fear,"

When he was challenged.   Lachlan Smith
Was down too late, and Ida with
An " I don't think I'll go to-day,"
Announced her wishes straight away.
   At half past ten the waggonette,
In which old Mr Forte had met
Professor Cobham, was brought round,
When he to his surprise profound
Perceived that though a hot wind blew
(The Fahrenheit marked 92°)
With most oppressive sultriness,
Lil had exchanged her cool white dress
For a black silk with pannier
And flounce, and other heavy gear,
And long tight gloves—such sacrifice
Will women make to touches nice.
She certainly looked very well,
And what the vulgar call ' a swell,'
But not so graceful or so bright
As in her simple dress of white.
However it would not have done
For younger sisters to have gone
Much dressed, while elder went arrayed
In simple fabrics simply made.
The gentlemen left in the lurch
(For want of space) all walked to church,
A pretty little bluestone pile
Which Mr Forte had built, with aisle
And nave and chancel.   It was decked,
With some fair notion of effect,
By Lil, and Maud, and Margaret.

The hymns to pretty tunes were set,
But like the sermon ill-prepared :
The gossips of the township stared,
As village gossips always will,
At Mrs Forte, and Maud, and Lil,
To criticize their looks and dress,
And comment on their ugliness :
And then the plate went round, and then
They shook hands and drove home again,
Along a heavy, sandy road,
While overhead a fierce sun glowed,
And the north wind with sudden gust
Caught up and eddied clouds of dust.
Arrived at home they came on Will,
And Kit, and Lachlan Smith, and Phil,
On sundry sofas lying prone,
And reading newspapers, alone,
In sheer disgust because the day
Was far too hot for tennis play.
Kit decked for dinner in a dress,
Cut with a habit's simpleness,
Made of black velvet, Will and Phil
In their old tweed shell jackets still.
The Christmas dinner was at two,
And all that wealth or pains could do
Was done to make it a success,
And marks of female tastefulness
And traces of a lady's care
Were noticeable everywhere.
The port was old, the champagne dry,
And ev'ry kind of luxury

Which Melbourne could supply was there.
They had the staple Christmas fare,
Roast beef and turkey (this was wild),
Mince pies, plum pudding, rich and mild,
One for the ladies, one designed
For Mr Forte's severer mind,
Were on the board.   Yet in a way
It did not seem like Christmas day,
With no gigantic beech Yule-logs
Blazing between the brass fire dogs,
And with 100° in the shade
On the thermometer displayed.
Nor were there Christmas offerings
Of tasteful inexpensive things,
Like those which one in England sends
At Christmas to his kin and friends,
Though the professor with him took
A present of a recent book
For Lil, and Madge, and Mrs Forte,
And though a card of some new sort
Had been arranged by Lil to face,
At breakfast, everybody's place.
  When dinner ended, nearly all
Stole off to have a snooze or sprawl
Upon the lounges in the hall.
The heat was too oppressive still
For outdoor exercise, but Will
Went out to give his dogs a run
In a plantation where the sun
And wind were broken by the trees.
And Kit, who bore the heat with ease,

Challenged Professor Cobham's skill
At billiards ; Hall, and Smith, and Phil,
Lazily blowing clouds of smoke,
And criticising every stroke.
Each of the players much surprised
The other,—Kit had not surmised
That the professor's play would show
Such mastery of " running through,"
So quick an eye and sure a hand,
Nor he that she had such command
Of check and screw, and would display
So much sound judgment in her play.
 And so the long close afternoon
To its late end dragged slowly on,
Without a breeze from morn to eve
The suffocation to relieve.
Sunset just took away the glare
But did not cool the heat-charged air,
And everybody in the house
Was glad when tea-time came to rouse
Their languid torpor and despair.
 Tea over, no one seemed to care
To face the hothouse atmosphere
Of the verandah, but drew near
To listen to Lord Chesterfield
And the Professor, who distilled
The pith of Schliemann's ponderous
And formidable " Ilios ;"
Holding the book up in his hand
To illustrate as he explained
That those who heard might understand

A heavy subject, at the best
By no means easy to invest
With any human interest,
A fact which was not lost on Kit,
Who hinted with her ready wit
That she would like it just as well
If he would close the book, and tell
Homeric tales, and make them rife
With touches of the old Greek life
As painted by the bard. "You can
Bear out or quarrel with Schliemann
By following his theories
Or choosing those which he denies,
And we shall have our tale, and learn
Greek habits without study stern."
The rest her action ratified,
And, as a subject she'd supplied,
Declared her Queen without resort
To Justice Ballot-box's Court.

ODYSSEUS IN SCHERIA.

From the first shimmer of the summer-morn
Upon the breeze's wings had there been borne
Such echoes as are heard about a quay
When a great ship is putting out to sea ;
And all day long down to the port had rolled
A stream of men bearing great store of gold,
And broidered raiment, swords with studded hafts,
And brazen vessels, fair as that which wafts

The incense-smoke from Delphi, and bright arms
Such as make manly men in war's alarms.
And King Alcinoüs stood upon the deck
Watching the lading, lest the crates should check
The crew in reaching forward with their oars
To waft Odysseus to the longed-for shores.
And then he turned home, meaning with high feast
To celebrate the parting of his guest,
And slew an ox to the cloud-gatherer Zeus.
Then those who in the palace had their use,
Roasted the thighs, and therewith made much mirth,
And, when they were well feasted, summoned forth
The gifted bard who pleased the multitude,
And by them was much honoured ; who renewed
A lay half sung upon an earlier day
That had pleased well.   And when that it was gay
Loud shouts of laughter through the courtyard rang :
But when the deaths of island chiefs he sang,
And island queens with thongs bound round their
        hands,
Driven with blows and shame to hostile lands,
The laughter died away and eyes grew dim.
Such mastery of song was there in him.

But one there sate, unchanging with the song,
And little noting aught, but all day long
Gazing with levelled glances at the west
To see the sun's tired horses sink to rest

Behind the hill of ocean.   For his cause
The sacrifice and song and feasting was ;
And yet he heeded to them least of all
Who were within Alcinoüs' palace-wall.
For he was thinking how that he should come
With no long-waiting to his island-home,
And queen and son, and flocks and herds and stead,
And whether he should find Laertes dead ;
Or that the Theban's shade had told him truth ;
And in his mind viewed pictures of his youth,
And the old life in Ithaca, before
He followed the Atridae to the war.
No ploughman wearied by his clodded shoon,
Towards the close of winter afternoon,
Could look unto the setting of the sun
With more of hope and welcome than this one.
And lastly the sun set : and then he spake
Unto the King, craving that he might take
His escort and his treasures, and all things
That the great gods, whose lot is above kings',
Had vouchsafed to him, to the hollow ship.
And then he spake, and this with trembling lip,
Of her against whose pure and wifely name
Envy itself had never whispered blame,
While she spun on through twenty widowed years,
And nightly washed her spinning out in tears.
And then he spake the word which those who rove
On pathless seas and sands, and exiles love—

"Home:" and then prayed that fair days should
   befall
His kindly host—good cheer within his hall,
Chaste wives and goodly children ; and then prayed
The God, who ever makes it his to aid
The suppliant and stranger, to rain down
All manner of good gifts upon this town,
And that no ill should come unto its folk
And take abode with them.

            And while he spoke
There was a hum of praise, and when he made
An end of speaking, all with one mind bade
That he should have his ship ; nor did the King
Dissent from what they willed, but, summoning
Pontonöus, the herald, bade him pour
Into the mystic graven bowl great store
Of sacred wine, and all the heroes call
Into the lofty roofed, bronze-paven hall,
That they might pray Zeus with a shielding hand
To bring the stranger to his fatherland.
And so it was—Pontonöus filled the bowl
With wine that soothed the sorrows of the soul,
And gave to each in order as they sate.
Who to the gods, that hold their solemn state
On the broad hill of heaven, duly poured
The first drops in libation, and implored
Safe conduct for the guest.   But he stood up

ʼAnd set in the Queen's hand a drinking cup
With double bowls set base to base, one full
And crowned with wreathing flow'rs and snowy wool,
And spake therewith such wingèd words to her—
"O Queen, I pray the gods to give thee cheer,
Until the fair day when old age and death
Come, as they come to all who draw our breath.
Nor do I think that age will come alone ;
For unto me thou seemest such an one
As are the blessed gods who wax not old.
And, but that I by Pallas had been told,
I had thought thee immortal, as they be.
Now I am going home.   Zeus prosper thee,
And leave thee long to have thy full delight
In King Alcinöus' heroic might,
And all thy children and the men, who love,
With oars too great for other folk, to rove
Over the open sea (whose waters shine
As darkly and as clearly as the wine
Crushed in the islands from the purple grape),
Delighting all these with thy queenly shape
And godlike wisdom. "

              And therewith he passed
Over the threshold of the doorway vast,
Led by the royal Herald to the quay,
Whereby the ship rode chafing for the sea,
And went aboard.   And the Queen's womenfolk

Brought him from her fair linen and a cloke
Fresh-washed but now, and the strong coffer faced
With plated bronze whereon Odysseus placed
A magic lock, which sunborn Circe wrought,
And with self-working understanding fraught;
Wherein were stored the princes' goodly gifts,
The talents of pure gold, the thirteen shifts
Of royal vesture, and the noble sword
Which Sir Euryalus brought forth from his hoard
Partly to do the bidding of the King,
And partly as his own free offering,
To soothe away the bitter words he spake ;
Goodly the weapon, and of wondrous make,
With biting blade and sheath of ivory,
Carven with curious myths of days gone by,
And silver studded hilt.   And there, too, lay
The wine bowl that Pontonöus yesterday,
And many a year before, had daily filled
With the sweet grape juice, when Alcinöus willed
To pour libations.   This the King had given
That whensoe'er Odysseus looked to heaven,
Sitting at sacred feast, he might recall
The lofty-roofed, bronze-paved, Phaeacian hall
And him who sate within it on his throne.
Made all of gold it was, with handles on,
And with a wreath of leaves of beaten gold,
And mingled golden roses round it rolled.

And others bare him ruddy wine and wheat ;
And when all things were brought, there sate at meat
Odysseus and the escort that he had ;
And, when all were with banqueting full glad,
Down in the hollow of the ship they made
Well in the stern a bed, and thereon laid
Soft cloths of wool and linen, that he might
Rest easy mid the rockings of the night.
And then with sound of flutes and many a shout
They from the capstan paid the cables out
Which moored the ship alongside of the quay,
And cast her out into the stream ; and she,
Unlike man's ship slow forging at the start,
Leapt straightway into swiftness like a hart,
Or like a four-horse chariot in the ring,
Or hawk that cleaves the wind on lightning wing.

And then with more of music and glad noise
(The while the seamen did the mainsail hoise)
The heralds took their way back to the house,
And mingled with the heroes in carouse.
But on the seashore, all alone, stood one
Who, with strained eyeballs, through the twilight dun
Scanned the dim form of the departing ship
Not without lashes moist and quivering lip ;
A maiden with her girlhood scarce outgrown,
Tall and still slender, with her brown hair done
Into a plaited coil, and with grey eyes

D

That had the clearness of the summer skies,
And something of their colour; her soft cheeks
Were tinted with the duskiness that speaks
Of sunny playhours and warm southern blood,
And yet when shame or dancing brought the flood
Of crimson to her face, the glow shone through
As fairly as through skins of fairer hue.
Robed was she in soft white, with but a braid
Of golden thread upon its border laid,
And with gold bosses on her sandal thongs,
And golden brooches with sharp pointed prongs
Buckling her peplus.

        She gazed on the ship
With moistened eyelashes and quivering lip,
Not that it bore away her hopes; they had
Been stricken over night, when all were glad
With the saved stranger's story, as he told
Of all his wars and perils manifold.
For therein had he spoken of his quest
To win to rocky Ithaca, and rest
In the chaste arms of his enduring wife.
And at that word there fell on her young life
A shadow such as falls upon the eve,
When the last glimmers of the sunset leave.
And yet the best of the Phaeacian land,
Great seamen, mighty chiefs, had sought her hand,
And wooed her pleasure many a day in vain,

And moved her not e'en so much as to pain
In the refusal, but were ever met
With a smooth, heedless smile and a "not yet."
Her wont and her delight had been to sport
Among the maidens of her mother's court,
At ball and dance, and music, and to play
With her own brothers, passionless and gay,
And light of heart, giving no thought at all
Unto the lot that uses to befall
King's daughters and fair women, as of fate,
When they have come to womanly estate.

And why should this man win so much on her?
He looked not like a lady's courtier
With his great shoulders, stoop, and weight of head
That his low stature nowise warranted.
Nor did he heed his person overmuch,
But let the sun and sea and weather smutch
His arms and face with brown, and let his hair
And beard curl and run riot everywhere.
Nor was he in the first prime of his age,
Nor were the nice tricks of a palace page
Observed in his grave manner and address;
Though there could not but be some courtliness
In one who had so much with outland men
Mingled as suppliant or alien,
Envoy or treaty-maker: nor had he,
At least as from his speech might gathered be,

Much heed for woman's beauty or fair ways,
But, speaking no great matter in their praise,
Dwelt much upon the palling of the love
With which Calypso, in her island-grove
Of poplar and sweet-scented cypress, strove
To move him to forgetfulness of home;
Love of a kind that surely would not come
To all men thus unwelcomely, but most
Would look upon it as the crown and boast
Of all their lives, and not, as this strange man,
Seek how he might by wile Dædalian
And prayer, and by entreaty face to face,
Win his way out from each delightful place
To sail back to his rocky heritage
And to a wife now well advanced in age—
If she indeed yet lived, and had not gone
To join the shades that flit about the throne
Of gloomy Dis, and thirst for draughts of blood.
Sated he seemed of all fair womanhood,
As though the spring of worship and desire
Had dried up in his veins, and all youth's fire
Had burnt away. And he spake wearily
Of pageants, revels, and court ceremony
And even the nymphs' gardens of delight—
Full of strange sweetnesses to charm the sight,
And scent, and hearing of all mortal men
Whom fate or some god brought within their ken.

But when he spake of battles or of ships
The whole man changed, and then from out his lips
Poured such a stream of burning, speechful words
That he who heard half saw the play of swords,
The whirl of javelins, the dinted shields,
The blood-drenched herbage of the battle-fields
Rutted by wheels, and spattered up by hoofs,
And strewn with garments slashed of divers woofs,
And mangled limbs, and corpses, and dead steeds.
Or if he did recount his mighty deeds
On shipboard and his wondrous voyages
To haunted isles and undiscovered seas,
One seemed to hear the stormwind piping loud
About the rigging, and each stay and shroud
Groaning with ev'ry straining of the mast
As the great sail bent it before the blast,
And hear the ebb-wave rippling round the prow
When the shipmen had anchored from the bow ;
To see strange shapes of trees with naked stems
And cloud-high tops crested with diadems
Of giant flow'rs, and fruits, and spiky leaves ;
And see vast serpents and wild, humpbacked beeves
With manes like lions, and huge, fire-bright birds
With monstrous bills that shrieked out sounds like
    words
Or mocked with human laughter. And he told
Of that which, neither beast nor fish, is rolled
In armour of such proof as neither spear

Nor sword can pierce and armed with triple tier
Of jagged teeth, as great in length and mouth
As are the dread sea monsters of the South.
And then, perchance, of the dwarf, hairy men
That lived in trees and spake not back again
When they were hailed, but fled with savage screams
Deeper into the forest, bridging streams
With their own bodies linked by sorcery
And cunningly swung over from a tree.
These had he told and much more : and the maid
Hung on his lips while he his tale displayed,
Nor ought of the man saw she but did grow
Into proportion.   In his form did glow
The ravager of Troy, the voyager,
The nymphs' beloved, the Cyclops' vanquisher.
And then her thoughts fell back and she built up
The magic golden palaces of hope,
Laid lately in the dust, of words of praise
Breathed through a rain of kisses, and fair days
Beside him in the lofty bronze-paved house,
And great sons many wise and valorous
Reflecting back their father's praise on her
As he did on his mother.   Then some cheer
Came to her, calling back the gracious words
He spake to her when the Phæacian lords
Had left them, giving her the thanks and love
For his saved life.   And then again she strove
To unbuild the fabric gently, course by course,

But fell to weeping tribute to remorse,
And listening to the sad throb of the tide
Until she wept to sleep by the seaside.

The narrative was hardly o'er
When all were startled by the roar
Of thunder-claps right overhead,
And by a lightning fork which shed
A flash of light as broad as day
Over the hall, with its clear ray
Illuminating every nook,
Leaving the ladies terror-struck,
Excepting Mrs Forte, and Kit
Who went outside to look at it.
Peal after peal and flash on flash
Seemed to portend the instant crash
Of roof and chimney-stack and wall,
And swift destruction to them all.
But the Professor, who had gone
Outside with Kit to look upon
The glory of the storm, could see
No shadow of anxiety
Or fear upon her proud fair face
When sometimes for a moment's space
'Twas lit with the electric gleam.
  Now meanwhile it began to seem
To those inside in their suspense
As if the atmosphere intense
Would suffocate them even though
They were not crushed at one fell blow,

For not a single drop of rain
Had fallen, though the hurricane
Raged with such fierceness o'er the plain.
But at the last, with rushing sound
And dashing huge Gums to the ground,
· Came the rain squall through the tree tops,
At first with huge infrequent drops,
Then in a deluge pouring down
Like waterfalls upon the crown
Of mountain-gorges when the snow
Beneath the sun's increasing glow
Is melted on the Alpine peaks,
While valiant Kit, whose rosy cheeks
Had blenched not at the storm, was fain
To flee in rout before the rain,
Which gave way to an icy chill
And hailstones huge enough to kill
Such hapless bird or animal
As in their path might chance to fall.
  Soon as the rain began to pour,
The thunderstorm passed quickly o'er,
And with it fled the stifling heat,
Leaving the air quite fresh and sweet,
Which tempted most of them to walk
Out in the air to smoke or talk,
All save the two old folks and Lil,
Who made their hearts expand and thrill
By playing snatches slow and clear
Of carols they'd been used to hear
Some half-a-century ago
At High Wick Manor, when the two

Were lad and maiden ; they talked on
Of England and what they had done
On bygone Christmas nights at home,
Of friends beyond the northern foam,
And friends beyond that other sea
Yet further—whither ceaselessly
Travellers follow the old track,
But whence no messenger comes back.
  Outside, the conversation turned
On the same subject.   Cobham learned
That Chesterfield, although in truth
Colonial-born, had passed his youth
And boyhood in the mother-isle,
Had been at Westminster awhile
And Cambridge, which however he
Had left too soon for a degree,
And so the two had much to say
About the good old English way
Of keeping Christmas—carols, waits,
Yule logs, a furbishing of skates,
A hanging up of mistletoe
O'er spots where everyone must go,
And decorating church and house
With holly, presents numerous,
And Christmas-boxes, boxing-day,
With opening theatres gay,
And Twelfth-night with its " characters,"
And Twelfth-cake.   Kit to their converse
Listened attentively, and walked
In silence with them as they talked.
She took uncommon interest

In everything that was possessed
Or done by England. Englishmen
Of good position first, and then
Great English ladies, habits, sport,
And etiquette. Old Mr Forte
Had been her chief authority,
But he was half-a-century
Behind the latest. Now she had
One, not long since an undergrad.
In a crack Oxford College, near
To question on the social sphere
Of English gentry. So these three,
For half-an-hour it may be,
Walked up and down, till Mr. Forte
Called the Professor to support
Some view of English Christmastide,
Which Mrs Forte and Lil denied;
And there he stayed and talked at first
With the old people till he durst
Steal off to Lil, who sat alone
At the piano, mute anon,
Then symphonizing. She had been
In the late elemental scene
More terrified than all the rest,
But Cobham in his heart confessed
That on the whole he'd rather have
A girl too timid than too brave,
And that a gentle helplessness
In petty cases of distress
Affords a pretty patronage
For ladies—to a certain age.

His fancy certainly was struck
More with Lil's terror than Kit's pluck.
She looked so tender in her fright,
With quivering lips and cheeks blenched white,
And nervous hands clasped in dismay,
While there was, as the Scots would say,
A something unco' in the pride
Which thus the elements defied,
In one so young and exquisite
In woman's beauty as was Kit.

Boxing Day, December 26th.

All the young folks on Boxing Day
Were to go some ten miles away
To races held at Linlithgow,
A township with a hut or two,
A state school and a public-house
Of functions rather various,
Post office, tavern, forge, and store.
   Will said at breakfast, " Four or more
Will have to ride, the waggonette
Although it's pretty roomy, yet
Can't very well accommodate
More than the luncheon-things and eight.
Butters will ride on just ahead
To let us through the gates, and spread
The tablecloth and knives and forks,
And open tins and draw the corks.
Who is for riding? "   " I," said Phil,
And Albert Hall and Kit and Lil,
And the Professor, who confessed
That his seat was not of the best,
And asked to have a quiet horse.
Will answered gracefully, " Of course
I never give a horse that kicks
Or 'bucks' or has uncertain tricks
To any man until I ken
How he can ride, and never then

Unless he asks me, or we're short
Of nags.   I think the so-called sport
Of putting new-chums on a brute
That bucks is cowardice absolute.
I don't think that we have a beast
About the place that bucks the least,
Except the grey Miss Johnstone picks.
Lil's chestnut shies but never kicks."
The riders started none too soon
At ten to reach the course by noon :
The ride itself amidst the trees,
Across bush paddocks, could but please.
But three at least of the cortege
Were chafing if not in a rage.
Not the Professor and not Kit,
Who rode exchanging shafts of wit,
And making the whole forest ring
With laughter blithe, or noticing
The glory of the summer morn
Through the thin gum-tree foliage borne,
But Phil and Lil and Albert Hall
Woefully disconcerted all
At this unlooked-for partnership.
Lil had looked forward to a trip
With the Professor tête-à-tête,
Knowing the admiration great
Her brother Phil had always had
For dashing Kit, since quite a lad,
And that the bushman in his way
Liked well enough with her to stay ;
And Phil and Hall had reckoned on

Choosing their own companion.
As Lil anticipated, they
From the Professor held away,
But then he was with Kit, not her,
And Phil had not a character
For taking disappointments well,
And muttered hints about 'a sell.'
And ladies Hall scarce understood
Unless they sunk their womanhood
In masculine proclivities.
And so they rode in silence wise
With ennui undiversified,
Save when Lil's horse was scared and shied
Because a wounded wallaby
Sprung almost at its feet to fly.
Her fearlessness and skill combined
Astonished those who thought to find
A timid rider in the form
Which cringed so from the thunderstorm,
And Cobham, as they rode behind,
Revealed to Kit his puzzled mind.
" Lil's a conundrum," answered she,
" She'll pick a snake up fearlessly
To dash its head against a tree,
And run in terror from a cow
As tame as those we passed just now."
   At length they rode up to the course,
An unfenced clearing where a horse
Could only know the track because
'Twas clear enough to let him pass.
A few drink-shanties and a box

Built for the judge of redgum blocks,
With sundry poor time-honoured shows
Alone beside the "paddock" rose
To stamp the race-course. There were few
Bookmakers, the bookmaking crew
Flying at higher game elsewhere.
The horsey, noisy talent here
Was chiefly local. Then there were
Owners of horses, stable boys
And station-hands, who made much noise
Of a good-humoured hearty sort,
And shewed keen relish of the sport,
But did not drink as people do
In England, or "knock down their screw"
For a whole year like those who've been
On far-back stations Riverine.
  Being bred up a Londoner,
Though he'd spent much of ev'ry year
Out in the country, Cobham knew
Little of horses but the two
That brought her carriage every day
To take his mother out, and they
When they had brought her home at night
Dropped as completely from his sight
Until the morrow afternoon
As if they stabled in the moon.
And therefore he paid far more heed
To lunch and lady than to steed,
But not to Kit instinctively,
For she had neither ear nor eye
For anything but boy and horse

When she was once upon the course,
And was so far preoccupied
As to let Phil usurp her side
And feast his eyes upon her charms
Without recourse to flight or arms.
　　It was not altogether chance
Or undesigned, the circumstance
That in their morning gallop there
Cobham had been Kit's cavalier,
For Kit, as has been said above,
Was a sworn Amazon, and love
Was not a topic she'd endure
From any man, nor was she sure,
What Phil's precise intentions were.
He certainly bestowed on her
More of his company and care
Than he was wont to give the fair,
And she had seen him more than once
Dart her a glance that might announce
A state of feelings that would be
Distasteful in the last degree,
If he were to interpret it
As seemed most likely to her wit.
And if they'd ridden tête-à-tête,
And then had chanced to separate
From their companions as they rode
Through the lone paddocks, with their blood
Excited by the exercise
And storm-cleared atmosphere, Phil's eyes,
Might have been warmly seconded
By words she'd rather keep unsaid,

And so she had condemned poor Lil
To penance between Hall and Phil.
But Lil could have her full reward
When they were once upon the sward,
For the Professor, as was said,
Had not been in the country bred,
And about horses knowing naught
Had not the interest he ought,
And Lil, although she'd always been
Much among horses, yet had seen
So much of racing and the best
That she took no great interest
In a bush-meeting, unless one
Of her friends' horses chanced to run,
And then just for the minute's space
Of the duration of the race.
Besides she looked much prettier,
As the Professor could aver,
Than he had seen her look before,
With a fresh rosy tint spread o'er
Her cheek, which sometimes, he'd confess,
Was just a shade too colourless.
Then the swift motion through the air
Had loosened a bright lock of hair,
And as, if fault in her you'd find,
She was a trifle too inclined
To slenderness, a habit made
Of soft grey "homespun" tweed displayed
Her figure at its best—the fit
Perfect enough for even Kit.
    Lunch was a feature of the day,

Which Butters had been told to lay
As soon as he had fastened up
The nags and given them their sup.
The three seats of the waggonette
Could be detached, and they were set
Beneath a shady wattle tree,
So that each lady on her knee
Could take her lunch conveniently.
There was no lack of luxury,
For turkey, chicken, duck, and pie,
Were ranged before the luncher's eye,
Flanked with peach-tart, Madeira cake,
Plum pudding, shortbread (of Scotch make),
And summer fruit and clotted cream,
With champagne flowing in a stream
Exhaustless. Soon the ladies went
Satisfied to their heart's content,
Leaving their cavaliers at ease
To finish luncheon when they'd please.
The gentlemen had 'jolly fun,'
For they were hungry everyone
And in high spirits. Chesterfield
Had the consummate art, concealed
Beneath his kindness, to appear
Contented with whatever cheer
Was set before him ; honest Will,
Child-like, loved any outing still ;
And the Professor, for his part,
A boon companion was at heart.
     When they rejoined the ladies, he
Helped Lil to mount, a mystery

He did not clearly understand,
But took her dainty foot in hand
As cheerfully as if he knew
Exactly what he ought to do.
And then he mounted, and the two
Rode slowly round, outside the course,
Oblivious of friend or horse,
Until the crowd that went away
Proclaimed the finish of the day,
When they resought their friends in time
Not to be noticed much.   To climb
Unaided to her saddle took
Kit scarce a moment, then she shook
Her reins and cantered up to Lil
And Cobham, leaving Hall and Phil
To join the three or ride apart
Just as it pleased them—in her heart
Dreading a ride with Phil alone
A good deal more than she had done
Before he'd drunk so much champagne,
And striven with his might and main
To make her day enjoyable.
She had not liked it half as well
As she was wont, from constant care
Lest he should take her unaware
When none were near her, and intrude
The question she would fain elude,
Of which th' attentions he had paid
Gave her fresh cause to be afraid.
So she was forced for her own sake
Lil's tête-à-tête once more to break,

For, as she feared, esprit de corps
Or dread of being deemed a bore
Might make Hall spur his horse away,
If he thought Phil had aught to say.
   However, Lily Forte and she
Had wide enough diversity
In character to be fast friends,
And Kit strove hard to make amends
For her intrusion by the will
To set the Oxford man and Lil
Each in the other's graces good,
To take care that each understood
The other's merits. They went home
A good deal faster than they'd come,
And soon had cantered into view
Of Mr Forte's oak-avenue.
      *   *   *   *   *

Half way through dinner, Will had said
That, if objection no one made,
He voted that the tale should be
In the Verandah, so that he
And those who chose might have their smoke.
And very sensibly he spoke,
Since just as women like to sew
When they have nothing much to do,
But may not read or talk, so men
For their cigar or pipe are fain.
      *   *   *   *   *

They did not draw the lots because
It seemed too formal, but Lil was
By common acclamation named

Queen of the night, and, as such, claimed
Another tale of old Greek lore,
Such as he'd told the night before,
And asked him, if he could, to say
More of the sad Nausicäa.
Accordingly th' Oxonian,
Ere he the evening's tale began,
Repeated to them a sad song
That he had fancied for her tongue.

THE SONG OF THE LOVE-SICK NAUSICAA.

Doomed back again to the dull island life,
To be at best the oft-neglected wife
Of some sea-roving, rude Phaeacian.
Nor shall I hear the breakers plash, nor scan
One ship bound outwards in the twilight dim,
Without a pang of longing after him.

The island chiefs are seamen skilled and bold;
But when their feats in sea-craft have been told,
Their store of plundered wealth, their deeds of blood,
And some strange ventures on the Libyan flood,
There is not much made up unto their wives
For the unending sameness of their lives.

Had he but stayed, and had he not been wived,
How happy in his wedlock had I lived,
Watching him 'mid the heroes in the ring
Foremost in every art that fits a king,

And, when night drave us into the high hall,
Hearing fair words from out his wise lips fall,

Of how, beside their ships in front of Troy,
The common round of gain and strife and joy
For nine long years busied the Argive chiefs,
Varied with skirmishes and some few griefs,
As when a prince ventured in foraying
Too far, and fell to Paris's bowstring:

Then he would tell of that last crowning year
When all things boded that the end drew near,
Of Hector's death and Paris' poisoned wound,
And how the kindly Menelaus found
And took his fair wife to himself again;
And lastly of his own hap on the main,—

Of his escape from sunborn Circe's isle,
And from divine Calypso's love and guile,
Of Polyphemus and the Laestrygons,
And of the Sirens and the whitening bones—
His shipwreck, his stern struggle with the sea,
And how that he looked lovingly on me

From the first sight! How happy had I been
If fate had given me to be his queen,
To cherish him whose prudent counsels won
The overthrow of godlike Ilion,

Who hath been in his very miseries
The love of nymphs and care of goddesses !

But he hath passed away into the night,
Lost to our vision like the goodly light.
The light may come again on isle and sea,
But never the same perfect light to me,
In that my heart is darkened, and mine eyes
Will all things through his image see, veil-wise.

THE LEGEND OF HELEN AT SPARTA.

Helen, the daughter of King Tyndareus,
Or, as some say, of Ægis-bearing Zeus,
Had lived in Sparta many a goodly day
Ere the east wind blew down from Phrygia
Paris the fair, and many days lived she
In golden friendship free from taint, and free
With Paris and her husband afterward,
Until the son of Atreus went aboard
His swift black ship and sailed to far-off isles,
And there abode, leaving his wife long whiles
With Priam's godlike son (whether it was
By Aphrodite's lure, or for some cause
Of high state-policy or gain, or both).
The Queen to lose her lord was passing loath,
And fell to weeping, till the Phrygian
To soothe with words of comforting began,

And then was so insistent, that he must
Be as insistent to fulfil the trust
Of cherishing the dame, which the Greek King
Had laid upon his honour at parting,
In nowise dreaming of the afterhap
That Nemesis bare for him in her lap,
But full of tenderness for the young wife
Whom he was leaving, lest her daily life
Should be a prey to loneliness and tears,
And, as men oft in their preventing fears
Prevent their hopes, so did the Spartan King.
For, after the first days of sorrowing,
Helen began to look with grateful eyes
Upon his youth, who in such tender wise
Had healed her sorrows, nor was gratitude
Long ere it did descry in what it viewed
Fair lineaments and princely qualities,
Such as few men in any man despise,
And least of all a woman, who has been
Won by those very graces from her teen.
And thus these two lived joyously each day,
Wiling the swift-winged golden hours away,
Charmed by each other's gifts, as by a spell.
Helen, as woman, could but note too well
Him unto whom her least wish was a care
Like a behest from heaven, and compare
The goodliness of shape, the fair bright hair,
Fair face, swift feet, and skill in archery,

Which made him with far-darting Phœbus vie,
Against the simple worth of her own lord
Who, in the melée staunch and staunch in word,
Was yet none such as the Pergamian Prince,
Nor in such courtier-fashion could evince
The great, true love he bare her in his soul.
And, as for Paris, how should he control
His eyes from looking on the loveliness
That with its presence all his days did bless
And made his earth a heaven—not that he thought
In those first days of doing wrong in aught
Unto the son of Atreus; nor did he deem
That such things would be.   Nathless in a dream
It seemed that Aphrodite to him came,
And, garlanding a crown of amber flame
Around the sleeping princess where she lay,
Set him to thinking of that other day
When he bestowed the apple upon her,
And she on him had promised to confer
The fairest of fair women on the earth,
And set him thinking if for grace and worth
And tenderness and beauty and all love,
A goodlier dwelt e'en in the Paphian grove,
And set him thinking if it were not this
The goddess gave him in her promises.
And then he woke and to himself thus spake:
" Certes, great shame were on me did I break
The trust that Menelaus laid on me.

But he has passed over the pitiless sea
To far-off isles, and may not ever come
Back to the haven of his high-roofed home,
And meanwhile godlike Helen pines alone :
I cannot stay here always and anon,
When I have sailed she will be left a prey
To the rude chieftains, who will on her lay
Hot impious hands and hasten to divide
The kingdom as a spoil.   Better my bride
Were she than suffer such a cruel woe.
Yes ! Menelaus will not come back now,
Being so long gone, and I too must be gone,
Leaving the tender Queen thus doubly lone."
    With such and such words to himself he glozed,
While Helen on her lonely couch reposed
And dreamed ('twas Aphrodite moved the queen,
So sung old poets) of what might have been
Had she met Priam's son in the old days,
How what would now be shame might have been praise,
And she been wedded to this peerless knight
Bright in the hair, bright in the face, and bright
In all that fills a house with joy and light,
And yet no woman but an archer bold,
His own well able in the field to hold
With all the Spartan princes, and in speed
Matched to outrun the boar, if there were need,
On Mount Täygetus.   And then she woke
And chid herself for murmurs which she spoke

Unto herself while dreaming. But it chanced
That as she glid into the hall, she glanced
On Paris, while he chid himself likewise.
And lo it came to pass that when their eyes
Met, all the chidings vanished, and straightway
They thought but of the goodliness which they
Looked on in one another, and their hearts
Mingled, and, heedless of dread Hera's darts,
Who sanctifieth marriage, and the wrath
Of Menelaus, stepped on to the path,
Which leads through halls and gardens of delight
-Down to the black abyss, and on that night
And many another after, took deep draughts
Of passion's magic cup, until the shafts
Of Eos drove the friendly shades away.
    But last of all there came the hateful day,
Put back how often, when he needs must sail
Back to the Ilian shore, when favouring gale
And low waves and propitious augury
Conspired to bid the wanderer to sea,
And even Paris durst no longer stay
Lest Zeus himself should chafe at his delay.
And so he called his Trojans, and gave word
That on the morrow he would go aboard
And hoise sail for the Troad. Whereat they
Shouted with joy, seeing that many a day
It had been their desire once more to come
Unto the softer living of their home,

Its rich broad meadows and its goodly trees,
Its wealth and well-built houses ; for of these
Small store was there at Sparta, great and strong
In heroes as she was.   Then all day long
He and fair Helen gave themselves to love,
Although at first he took good heart and strove
To bid her his farewell, and swiftly go
Down to his ships to spread all sail and row
Beyond the reach of ill.   But still she clung
Close unto him, and on his shoulder hung,
And whispered that the summer sun was slow
In making home, and that fair winds would blow
For long days yet, and that the seas in June
Were softer than a summer afternoon.
Then wherefore haste to stand to sea that day ?
Or, if that day, why row the bark away
Before the sun's wrath softened and the eve
Stole down the sky the rowers to relieve
With calm and cool?   And even as she spake
She heaved up sighs as though the parting brake
Her heartstrings, and her white hands garlanded
About his neck, pressing her golden head
Against his shoulder lovingly.   But he
Read in his heart a sullen augury
Of threatening ill, and, deeming that he might
Avert their consummation by swift flight,
Turned a deaf ear to her most moving pray'rs,
And to assist the seamen in their cares

For watering and provision, forthwith passed
Down to his fleet black ship. But at the last,
When all things needful were within the hold,
In glitter of her beauty and red gold
Came peerless Helen, with a goodly train
Of virgins in bright raiment, Tyrian
Sea-purple or vermilion, whom she
Left standing by the ship's side on the quay,
And herself stepping on an outspread cloak,
Which one who seemed a ruler of ship-folk
Strewed for her slim, white, daintily-sandalled feet,
His homage with soft courtesy did greet,
And asked for Paris, safe voyage and God-speed
Wishing to bid him, and see if indeed
He was for sailing, and, when he had come,
Spake unto him of speeding to his home,
And, bidding him farewell in accents clear,
That all the folk who stood about might hear,
When they set up their din of loud applause,
Whispered to him to plead some specious cause
And stave the sailing off but for one day,
But for the night. Yet still he said her nay
In that he feared to. And then she again,
Seeing that Paris dared not to remain,
Gathered a desperate courage from despair,
And, flinging off all wifely shame and care
In the fierce love that lorded o'er her heart,
And, reckoning life naught should he depart

And leave her lonely in the bronze-sheathed house,
Whispered to him in accents tremulous
And passionate that, when she gave the word,
He should his faulchion draw and cut the cord
Which moored the ship and put straight out to sea
And carry her with him, and said that she
Would so dispose her train that none should be
Able to raise a finger in despite
When that she gave the signal for their flight.
And so it fell : for, bidding virgins twain
To stay by her, she bade the rest to gain
The homestead with all haste, and bring from thence
A milk-white steer with gilt horns and incense
For sacrifice and banquet, and rich wine
To win with gifts the clemency divine
Of King Poseidon, and to hold high feast
In honour of their parting, ancient guest.
And, when that they were gone, and as she thought
Come to the house, she turned about and sought
Paris, and he, although his heart waxed chill
Beneath the same presentiment of ill,
Bade to let go, and the huge galley leapt,
Like a loosed dog, from out the pier, and swept
With stately swing of deftly fitted oars
And swell of purple sails, and with bright spores
Of phosphorescent water sprinkled back
As the swift prow sped on its gleaming track,
And with rich strains of flutes and wafts of spice

Breathed from the poop moulded with some device
Of the Dædalian art, straight out to sea.
And those two sate together lovingly
Beneath an awning of thick web, with sides
Curtained from view, three golden eventides
And morningtides. And for the time great joy
Was theirs, but tempered with a dull alloy
Of aguish misgivings, and remorse,
Which sits behind the rider on the horse
Of pleasure when he tramples 'neath the hoofs
Another's paradise. And now the roofs
Upon the shore began to fade from view,
And they were left between the nether blue
And upper, without aught within their sight
To break the ring of azure, save the flight
Of wingèd fish escaping from the jaws
Of the bonitos to the expectant maws
Of hovering snowy sea birds, till the isles
With which the glorious Ægæan smiles
Fronted the flying bark, and made them heed
Unto their helm and move with minished speed.
And so they came to Troy one summer day,
And long whiles ere they passed right up the bay,
Through the shrouds looking, Helen did she list
Could see the shore's grey outline, dimmed with mist
As by a mist of tears or by a dream—
So in her ecstasy it well might seem.
But when they drew up to the quays of Troy

The city folk met them with hail of joy,
Seeing the well-known sails which they had deemed
Would never come again, and all men streamed
Down from the seaward gate unto the quay,
And women too, bareheaded, fired to see
The darling of their city once again,
Him who had been the brightest of all men,
Swiftest in chace, and surest with the bow,
And who had scouted every thought of woe,
Making the townsmen glad and of good heart,
Ready to play a gallant manly part,
On field or wall against the enemy.
This was the Paris of their memory,
Not like the after Paris, weak with sin,
Careless of all things so that he might win
Another hour with Helen, unashamed,
Though worsted in the fight, and world-wide blamed
As coward, miscreant, and city curse,
And basest knight of all the universe.

    And when they looked on Helen, every shout
Doubled itself and brought even elders out
To see what good it should be that could raise
An outburst so beyond the wont of praise.
Such infinite grace was in her visage seen
To gladden eyes of men, and all her mien
So gentle, godlike, marvellously bright,
That all their hearts clave unto her outright;
Nor did she ever fall from that high state,

But men were glad to meet their bitter fate
For her sake till the city fell.   Such love
Had the gods deigned her in all hearts to move.
   So they went up to Ilion, and the crowd
Followed with glee and joyous shoutings, proud
Of their long-lost and late-recovered chief
And his fair bride, and dreaming not that grief
Out of such joyful auspices should come.
And thus Queen Helen came to her new home.

   He ceased mid acclamation—all
   Listening to the fate and fall
   Of Helen with attention wrapt,
   And one there thinking how it happed
   That he had had a Helen too,
   A Helen who was fair to view,
   And loved by all who looked on her
   For womanly soft character,
   With woman's steel devotion mixed,
   And who her love unfaltering fixed
   On him, although he lived away
   For years as many as Greece lay
   Before the ramparts of Troy town,
   A Helen who had never known
   A Paris—with clear sapphire eyes
   Which never bent in loving wise
   On any eyes but his, with hair,
   So beautifully waved and fair,
   Which never felt a coaxing hand

F

Save his, who left her native land
To share his exile and new home,
And not, like the first Helen, roam
To leave her husband.   Helen Forte,
Wholly unconscious of the thought
Which flitted through her husband's brain,
Was thinking in a thankful strain
How merciful it was that she
Had ne'er been left by fate to be
Tempted like her fair eponym,
Not counting her long wait for him
As aught.   So potent is the spell
Cast over women who love well.
   Nor were the two old folks alone
Moved by the evening's tales, for one
Had listened to Nausicaa's grief
On learning that the island-chief
Was wedded, and would sail away
Not without picturing a day
When she herself might sadly gaze
Toward the dim horizon's haze.
This story of Nausicaa
Planted the embryo of dismay
In her soft heart, though she cared not,
So she assured herself, one jot
For the Professor.   Yet she knew,
And swiftly the conviction grew,
That did she learn that he was wed
A load of disappointment dead
Would press on her, that when he went
The gentle hours of content

Would take wing with him.   Margaret,
Although she understood not yet
Much of the meaning of the tale
Of Spartan Helen, did not fail
To sympathize with her as one
On whom much woe would fall anon.
And practical Maud Morrison
Made up her mind that she would ne'er
Herself as witlessly ensnare
As the Greek Queen pourtrayed therein,
The type of beauty in soft sin,
With no fault but her frailties,
To bards of thirty centuries.

   *   *   *   *

The dancing flagged that night because
Phil, who had waltzed with scarce a pause
On yule night with Maud Morrison,
Was so unsettled by the tone
Kit had maintained while going to
And coming back from Linlithgow,
Though she was his companion
Through the delicious afternoon,
That he was fain to spend the night
In hanging by her side to right
That which was keeping them apart,
Not knowing in his blinded heart
That he was wooing his ill-fate
By striving to ingratiate.
" Leave well alone " 's a proverb old,
And truly, if the truth were told,
" Leave everything alone " should be

A proverb too.   The more that we
Multiply schemes and work we do
Multiply our misfortunes too.
The worst misfortunes of my life
I've brought down on my head by strife,
To lessen or to obviate
Misfortunes of a lighter weight
Which I anticipated and
Which would have, had I held my hand,
By a mysterious Power, been
Diverted from me (as I've seen
By the event).   And thus poor Phil
Forced on his crisis.   Pretty Lil
And the Professor somehow found
That although waltzing round and round
Has its own pleasures, maid and man
By sitting still together can
Equal, if not more joy obtain :
So they too left the mazy train,
And as young ladies entertain
A fear that if, e'en once they let
A man not in their dancing set
Dance with them much, because there are
None of the real caviare
At hand, they afterwards may find
The barrier thus undermined
Hard to shore up to its old strength,
Poor Maud was satisfied at length
That she would have no dance that night :
So, wearing an expression bright
Which did not in the least express

Her frame of mind, she went to press
Her services on Mrs Forte
As the musician, cutting short
Remonstrance with insistance stern
That she must be allowed her turn
Or could not bear to dance again.
A threefold end did she attain
By this manœuvre. Firstly, she
Did honestly desire to be
Considerate; and secondly,
It saved her having to comply
With undesirable requests
For dances, which good taste's behests
Would not permit her to refuse;
And thirdly, 'twould be an excuse
If while she stayed there, she should chance
Again to deprecate a dance.
And further she could play so well
That, like most people who excel,
It flattered her to thus display
Her skill. And playing chased away
The demonry of jealousy
Which haunted her when Phil stood by
The Queenly Kit, who, ill at ease
With his mistimed attempts to please,
Was scarce her royal self that night,
Though she made some few sallies bright,
But occupied with all her strength
In keeping him at sword-arm's length.
The dancing lapsed, and left therewith
Maud to the clutch of Lachlan Smith,

And Hall and Will in sheer despair
Taking to billiards ;—the whole air
Was thundercharged with discontent.
  Meanwhile the very contrast lent
Fresh graces to the laughing girl,
Baring a gleaming rim of pearl
At each fresh anecdote and jest
Related to her with such zest
By the Professor, who began
To feel himself a happier man
When good hap let him wile away
An hour alone in converse gay
With this warm-hearted gentle fay.
  It certainly beatifies
Those who are not too worldly-wise
To have bright tender maiden's eyes
Sharing one's gaze at everything,
And white hands always dallying
Before one ; and it pleases well
If, when one has a tale to tell,
A pretty Lil with little ear
Is stretched on the " qui vive " to hear
Each word one says ; nor does one's mind,
If not too seriously inclined,
Object to a companion graced
With girlhood's flower, summer-faced
And sunny-haired and fairy-light,
Though not below the middle height.

December 27th.

Last night before they went to bed
A picnic they'd determinèd
Into the forest, some to seek
A dish of yabbers* from the creek,
And some to gather maiden-hair,
And some to shoot and some to share
In laying lunch and brewing tea.
Phil drove the buggy, and much he
Entreated Kit his mate to be,
Which, seeing that it held but two,
She steadily refused to do ;
And as his pride would not submit
Beside her in a trap to sit
With any driving but his own,
He had to take Maud Morrison,
Only too pleased to have the chance
Of watching two swift ponies prance
Before a deft whip, while she sate
With her prime favourite tête-à-tête.
A thorough bushman, Albert Hall,
Had scarce been lured to go at all,
He'd too much of the real thing
To care about this picnicing.

* Yabbers are small fresh water cray fish rather larger than
prawns.

He liked to picnic on a chair
At table with a dinner fair,
And would have not gone had not Kit,
Gauging him with a woman's wit,
Offered her horse, the fiery grey,
Which she on the preceding day
Had mastered with such horsemanship
And without martingale or whip.
For well-contested stand-up fight
'Twixt man and horse was his delight,
And much of it was waged in sight
Of one or other, because Will
Had asked him to keep up until
All gates were passed.   Their road at first
Lay between paddocks interspersed
With few trees, rung,* and mostly dead ;
But when some miles were passed it led
Into a forest track which oft
Was block'd with " tea-tree bottom" soft
Or fallen trunk, compelling them
To make detours, and thrice a stem
Some inches through had to be topped,
Or they would have been wholly stopped.
Kit eyed the "new-chum" carefully
To see if he was scared thereby,
But when her gaze upon him turned
She found him wholly unconcerned.
He had gone up in her esteem
Because, although he did not seem
Well used to horses, yet he shewed

* Rung, *i.e.*, ring-barked.

So much nerve when he drove or rode.
  Will drove, and the Oxonian
Shared the box-seat with her, to scan
Whate'er there was of scenery,
Or unfamiliar to the eye.
Kit drove upon the road and track,
But, when they left it, Will took back
The reins, because he knew the lie
Of gaps in the vicinity.
Inside were Lil and Margaret
And Lachlan Smith on one side set,
And on the other Chesterfield
And Mrs Forte and Ida pealed
Glad laughter.   So they came at last
To where a muddy creek ran past
An open space, of brushwood clear,
Where they could kindle without fear
A fire to boil the " billy " on.
Here Phil Forte and Maud Morrison
Were camped already—Phil, in spite
Of his first disappointment, bright.
Maud was so pretty, and then she
Snubbed many men so ruthlessly
That preference from her conferred
A kind of honour.   She had heard
His overtures by Kit declined
And had forthwith made up her mind,
If he asked her, to exercise
Her repertoire of witcheries
To make him in his own despite
Enjoy himself—and won the fight.

It took Hall some time to enforce
Complete obedience from his horse,
But then the noble beast confessed
The masterhand and ceased contest.
When he arrived he volunteered
To go with any who preferred
Shooting to fishing.   Only one
Went with him, Lachlan Smith—the gun
Was the Professor's, which he'd brought
In case some specimen he sought
Flew by him.   The young barrister
Quite equalled any Londoner
In cockneyism, though he was
Australian-born, and gave Hall cause
To take the gun for all their sakes,
In terror at his wild mistakes,
Upon the pretext (which was true)
That the great common cockatoo,
Which Lachlan wanted most to shoot,
Was a most shy and wary brute,
Till one was wounded and its cries
Brought others round to sympathise.
   " Give me the gun," he said, " and I
Will sneak along until I spy
One within easy shot.   My eye
Will note them much more easily
Than yours."   And then he plunged into
The scrub and soon was lost to view.
He had not fired a single shot
When he returned, though in one spot
A huge black snake he'd seen as near

As horn to horn upon a deer.
He'd passed it lest the gun's report
Should scare the birds and spoil his sport.
So wholly was he without dread
Of what, had he not been bush bred,
Might have appeared like courting death.
'Twas fortunate that he not Smith
Came on it.   What that legal sun
In his excitement might have done
Made the stout bushman shudder more
Than coming on black snakes, a score.
    The ferners too had seen a snake,
A small one, which contrived to make
Escape into its hole unhurt.
Chesterfield's nails were full of dirt
But he and blue-eyed Margaret
And Mrs Forte had not as yet
Much else results for toil to show,
Though Albeit, when they told him so,
Plunged back into the scrub and brought
An armful of *the prize* * they sought,
With roots attached and fronds as large
As oak-ferns grow beside the marge
Of dripping rocks and welling rills,
Beneath the blue Dumfriesshire hills.
    Ida was cook and parlour-maid,
And with Will's help the lunch-cloth laid,
But not the luncheon : for the ants
Were eager as annuitants,
As, not to be particular,

* A curious and rather rare variety of " Maiden-hair."

Ants in Australia always are.
In fact, the ant has far more right
To have its portrait opposite
The picture of the kangaroo
Upon our Arms than the Emu,
In that the latter every year
Less and less commonly appear,
A statement which does not apply
To the ant's busy family.
Will lit the fire, and Ida boiled
The tea and the potatoes spoiled,
Which in the ashes were to be
Toast-roasted so deliciously.
  In the meantime the other five
Were catching stores of " fish-alive,"
That is to say that two were, Lil
And the Professor.   Kit and Phil
And Maud were far too worryish
To do much good at catching fish,
Proving the proverb's truth and fun
That " two are company, three none."
For Phil Forte wished Maud Morrison,
Who, as his drive's companion
Had wooed him so engagingly,
Right at the bottom of the sea,
Or anywhere but where she was,
And Maud at all events had cause
To wish Kit anywhere but there,
While Kit would rather that the pair
Would take themselves post haste elsewhere
And let her fish escape at will

In trying to escape from Phil.
    But meanwhile, higher up the stream
Lil and her partner, in a dream
Of happiness, could scarcely pull
Their lines up fast enough, so full
Of yabbers seemed the creek where they
Had pitched their quarters for the day.
Their plan was simple and complete,
To tie a piece of lean raw meat
To a long stick, and leave between
A yard of string, and when they'd seen
Their quarry strike to raise the bait,
And a land-net insinuate
Behind the yabber, which darts back
Whenever it suspects attack.
    Lil taught the piscatorial art,
And the Professor lent his heart
As well as his intelligence
To mastering its rudiments.
He tried the baits, she used the net
With practised skilfulness, and met
With most unqualified success
Till luncheon came compassionless.
    The lunch was hardly packed away
When picnic-making for the day
Was stopped most unexpectedly
With heavy rain. The morn was dry,
And not a sign of rain had there
Appeared on the barometer,
And when they reached the house again
They found that not a drop of rain

Had fallen on the open plain,
Thus showing how undoubtedly
Forests attract humidity.
    Maud Morrison, in angry fit
At Phil's neglect of her for Kit,
Said she preferred the waggonette,
And so it fell to Margaret
To soothe his temper through a drive
Of miles not less than twenty-five,
Soaked to the skin before the start,
And with a big lump in her heart
Of pity for her brother's woe,
Which every one divined although
No one had put the thought in words.
If gaudy feathers make fine birds
There were no fine birds present there
Excepting Lil, and her welfare
Was due to the Professor's cloak,
Which he, accustomed to the soak
So imminent on any day
In Cumberland or Galloway,
Had, mid much laughter, stowed away
Before he left, beneath a seat.
Now he reaped thirty-fold, so sweet
Looked a fair face amid the tweed,
And gratitude for his kind deed.
    Her mother too escaped the whole
Beneath a cotton parasol,
The food for many a biting jest
When she for its inclusion pressed
(To save her from the sun, not rain).

The sunshine soon revived again
Kit's dress of 'homespun' cheviot:
But all that sun could shine could not
Restore the cherry and pale blue
Washed from their sashes broad into
Ida's and Maud's white dainty skirts,
Or heal irreparable hurts
In outraged ostrich-feathered hats,
With plumes reduced from rounds to flats.
  They meant to start at half-past four,
But started back two hours or more
Before the time, because the rain
Fell too hard-for them to remain.
And thus the clock shewed scarcely five
When they passed up the carriage drive.
  So tennis was proposed, and Will,
Giving him credit for more skill
Than he, at any rate, possessed
When out of form, politely pressed
The Oxford man to form a set
With him, his brother Phil and Kit,
Assigning him, as most expert,
To Kit, whose pride was nowise hurt
By the insinuation thus
Launched at her tennis genius
By Will unwittingly.   But they
Proved quite unequal to the fray,
As all thought likely.   Phil could play
A ' finished' game, with 'low return,'
And ' service' regular and stern,
Dealt 'overhand' and much neat 'cut,'

While Will excelled in 'reach' and 'put,'
And had he practised with his peers
Need certainly have had no fears
From Phil, though Phil was champion
That year in Melbourne. But Phil won
Set after set whene'er they played
Against each other, for he made
Fewer mistakes, and seldom gave
A 'loose-ball' quarter. Kit was brave,
But soon perceived the hopelessness
Of winning even scant success,
Though the Professor now and then
Fairly out-paced her countrymen
With a half volley quick and low,
Which few lawn-tennisers can do
Who were not racquet-bred in youth,
And he could give more 'cut' in truth
Than Phil himself, but then he 'served'
So many faults that he observed
That if 'cut' only won the day
He might be somewhere in the play,
But while returning 'overnet'
And into 'court' won ev'ry set,
He would have hardly any chance
With Phil's cool, well-timed elegance.
Kit, for a lady, played with skill
Hardly inferior to Phil,
'Served' well and 'took her balls backhand
And front' with wonderful command,
And 'cut' well: her great weakness lay
In her not 'getting back' to play

A fast ball 'volleyed' straight at her.
  After the first set it was clear
That she must play with Phil to make
An even match, which for all's sake
Was better.   The Oxonian
Was much ashamed to be the man
To spoil a lady's game, and Phil
Had sulked at being given Will
Instead of Kit.
                    The other court
Had Lachlan Smith and Lily Forte
On one side, and Maud Morrison
And Chesterfield in union
Upon the other.   Neither he
Nor Smith played very skilfully,
And he was much the worst.   Howe'er
His partner did not seem to care,
Although she hated as a rule
One who was clumsy or a fool.
In truth most girls it gratifies
To have the chance to patronise
A man so marked in any walk,
As to attract the great world's talk.
She herself played lawn tennis well,
Though she did not like Kit excel.
And though Lil, when she played her best,
Played better, but then Maud possessed
So much more self-reliant 'pluck'
That in a match, without good luck,
Lil would succumb submissively.
Maud took her cue with rapid eye,

G

And, seeing that they could not win,
Determined lightly to give in
In play, and her whole strength to wield
In fascinating Chesterfield.
When they had done one set they went
To watch the other tournament,
Which in the time was almost through
The last game of set number two.
    Will, who had noticed Lachlan Smith
Looking at the Professor with
A glance of scorn and pity mixed
At his mis-strokes, was so much vexed
That he invited him to be
His partner in set number three,
At the same time inviting Kit
And Phil, who entered into it
Most thoroughly, with telling glance
To make him rue the circumstance,
Which they did, playing every ball
Hard back to him, till his downfall
Was rendered final and complete
By Will's suggesting that the net
Might suit him better, where the two
Bade fair to beat him black and blue
With well-directed volleyings.
Nor was the altered state of things
Unpleasing to the other set
Where Lil and the Professor met
In fascinating rivalry,
Each wishing to be outdone by
The rival. Lil looked prettier

For the excitement and the stir
As she did ever, when there came
Into her cheeks the rosy flame,
The charm she most lacked : and the game
Served to display the native grace
Of all her motions, while her face
Was wreathed in smiles which now gave place
To merry laughter, now were still
Because a stroke taxed all her skill.
      *   *   *   *

When from the dinner they withdrew
The audience was less by two,
For Phil and Hall had sauntered out
To smoke and chat and stroll about,
Liking their own society
Better than sitting idly by,
While the Professor on demand
Told what they scarce could understand,
And did not care for in the least.
And even Will was ill at rest,
Although he thought it impolite
Not to be present.   On that night
Ida was chosen queen, but said,
That as a queen already had
Thrice worn the crown, 'twas time for it
Upon three gentlemen to sit,
And acclamation hailed the thought
And chose the host first, who besought
The story-teller for a tale
Romantic and historical.

THE LAST OF THE BRITONS, OR THE LEGEND
OF DUNMAIL RAISE.

Round Grisedale's mountain-girdled mere
The latest moon of all the year
Lights in its wane an ancient host,
Each warrior an armour'd ghost,
Arm'd with the arms our country bore
E'er its first foeman touch'd its shore :
Of bronze their sword, of flint their spear,
Their leathern shield a hide of deer,
A British host, the last that held
The land, that all was theirs of eld.
    Ten hundred years scarce pass'd away
After that first great Easter-day
E'er not a Keltic lord was known
Through all the coasts of Albion,
Save in the stormy hills of Wales,
And Cornwall's mines, and Cumbria's dales,
    And Mona's citadel ;
And Saxon was in league with Scot
From this his last and best lov'd lot
    The Briton to expel.
Then all at once the loyal men
Of Cymri leapt from rock and glen
    To join their king Dunmail ;
From saddle-back'd Blencathra's height,

Where, hidden from the sun's good light,
    The tarn they call Bowscale
Reflects the stars at middle day,
While in its depths unfathom'd play
    That strange immortal twain,
The only fish in this wide earth
That liv'd at our Redeemer's birth :
    They know not death or pain,
But live until he comes again,
For they, they only, did remain
    Of that world famous seven
Wherewith the ' Lord of Life ' did feed
Those thousands four—this precious meed
    To them alone is given.
At once did Cumbria's noblest pour
From all the peaks of huge Skiddaw,
From Skiddaw's cub, since called Latrigg,
From Windermere and Newby Brig.
High in the west from grim Sca'fell,
And wild Wastwater's lonely dell,
The dalesmen hurried down to bring
Arms, few but faithful to their king.
High in the east along that road,
The highest ever built, they strode :
And not a few from Langdale Pikes,
And Furness Fells and Furness Dykes,
    Which now the sea doth hold,
But flocks and beeves and giant trees,

And corn that shimmered in the breeze,
    Held in the days of old.
Ten thousand—good men all, and true—
Came where his royal standard flew,
    To fight for hearth and home ;
A home they'd held a thousand years
'Gainst Dane and Saxon, and the spears
    E'en of Imperial Rome.

Hard by Helvellyn's mountain-steep,
Where Leathes' mere begins to peep,
Rises a knoll, in later days
Call'd in the dale King Dunmail's Raise.
Here 'neath the mountain's shoulders sheer
The road that runs from Windermere
Is one long hill from Grasmere shore
To Wy'burn town, six miles or more.
In such a pass three hundred men
Might drive ten thousand back again :
Upon this rise did Dunmail post
His faithful, but too scanty, host.
But what avails devotion high,
Or chivalrous fidelity,
When tenfold is the foeman's rank,
And pouring in on front and flank.
'Twas thus that royal Dunmail's might
Was shattered in that fatal fight ;
For while ten times ten-thousand men,

The Saxon host, charged up the glen,
Down huge Helvellyn's rugged side
Pour'd the fierce Scot as pours the tide
Of some long-prisoned mountain stream
When broken is th' opposing beam
That damm'd its flood and turn'd its flow
To drive the miller's wheel below;
Or like the Cyclon blasts that sweep
Over the face of India's deep.
The Briton bravely met the charge
With levell'd spear and sturdy targe :
But vain—for, hemm'd on every hand,
Nought could avail the gallant band :
Not all the valour and the might
Of Arthur and each boasted knight
  Nam'd of the Table Round ;
Not all King Charlemagne's array
Of Paladins that on a day
  A grave with Roland found.

 A fiercer charge—his host gives way,
And Scot and Saxon fierce to slay ,
Cut down the Britons man by man,
Till scarce a tithe of all the clan
Fight their way through to tell the tale
And save the crown of King Dunmail.
For he has lost his faithful brand,
And now is in the foeman's hand,

With both his sons, ill-fated three,
Doom'd to a conqueror's cruelty,
Their only crime that they did fight
To keep the realm that was their right.
Bound hand and foot with cords they lay
Until the ending of the fray
Should give their conqueror liberty
To revel in his cruel glee.
Then—such the custom of his day—
With his own hand does Edmond slay
The sire before the children's eyes
And blinds them soon as e'er he dies.

The Britons who escap'd the fray
Hid on the hills till close of day,
Then dug a grave twelve fathoms deep
And laid their monarch down to sleep,
And rais'd a cairn of boulders high
In homage to his memory:
Then wended in procession drear
To hide his crown in Grisedale mere.
With weapons fiercely clench'd they strode
Three miles along the Grasmere road,
Until they came to Grisedale burn,
And up the Faery glen did turn:
Awhile upon Seat-Sandal pause,
Then slowly wind through Grisedale Hause
Down to the mere and through the crown

Where Dollywaggon Pike sheers down.
Fierce was the wave and fierce the storm,
And mist-besieg'd the mountain's form;
The Spirits of the Lake and hills
Were anger'd at their country's ills,
Anger'd that stranger-hands had ta'en
The Briton's last, best loved domain.
That night o'er forest, lake, and fell
Resounded many a ghostly yell;
Around Helvellyn's giant man
With threat'ning glare the marsh-fire ran.
In becks, that yester summer's night
Scarce trickled down in shallows bright,
By deep and furious floods were borne
Great rifted rocks and trees uptorn:
The wind that scarce was heard at noon
Roared like an Indian typhoon,
And westward over Langdale Pikes
The breakers fell on Furness Dykes,
And with one wild tremendous sweep
Encompass'd in their greedy deep
Tree, corn and cot, and grassy down
From Lancaster to Barrow town.
And by the forked fire from heaven
The oldest Druid oak was riven.
The oak-tree gods might reign no more
Upon their native Britain's shore,
But now must fly, to stay awhile

In mother Mona's magic isle,
And thence be driven in wild unrest
For ever further, further west.
Till, when five hundred years were gone,
The land that tombs the setting sun
Should feel the conquering foot of Spain ;
Then, ousted from their home again
With other byegone godheads lie
In Limbo to eternity.

The Britons ere the day was light
Scal'd the o'erhanging mountain-height,
And climbing, just as dawn began,
Held council on Helvellyn' Man.
Full little did they deem that night
That ev'ry eve, ere dawn was bright,
Their souls must go to Dunmail's cairn
And through the glen to Grisedale tarn ;
Then over Dollywaggon seek
The high Helvellyn's highest peak.
Yet so it is—for there are souls
Whom some almighty hand controls
To haunt some too-eventful scene,
Where in their lifetime they have been ;
Nor ever rest within their tomb
Until they have fulfill'd their doom :
The souls of all who've follow'd Cain,
The souls of all by murder slain,

Until the murderer pay the due
For him that fell and him that slew ;
The soul of him whose life was ill,
Who perish'd unrepentant still,
And him who treasure has conceal'd,
Until his treasure be reveal'd.
And so it is that Dunmail's host
Still haunt the battle-field in ghost.
Did they but deign betray their trust
Their souls might rest in hallow'd dust,
But while they guard their monarch's crown
May never to their tomb go down.
And so each day from fall of night
Until the morrow-morn is bright,
Through Grisedale-pass that ghostly clan
March grimly to Helvellyn Man.
And ev'ry night from Grisedale tarn
They bring a stone to Dunmail's cairn,
To show their sovereign that still
They're faithful to his royal will :
And when the cairn doth reach as high
As Dunmail 'neath the earth doth lie,
Once more shall be his flag unfurl'd
For the great Battle of the World,
For that great battle that must be
Before the day of Equity
When ev'ry man shall have his own
Each proud usurper overthrown,

When Israel shall reign once more
Upon the promised country's shore,
And Cossack, Georgian, and Pole
Be freed from Muscovite control.
Then Dunmail with his British spears
Again shall sally from the meres,
And free his own, his native land
From Saxon, Dane, and Norman hand.
From southmost Cornwall to Carlisle,
From Mona to the Kentish Isle
The Cymri, as in days of yore,
Shall rule our land from shore to shore ;
And all the Cymri clans bow down
Before the might of Dunmail's crown ;
The crown that erst in Grisedale's deep
His trusty host did nightly keep,
Now, after many a hundred years,
Again upon his head appears.
But never shall appear again
The gods that ruled our island then ;
Their day is past, their oaks are fell'd
In which their ritual was held.
No other gods shall be adored
Through all the earth but Judah's Lord,
And they be in that lifeless spot
For ever and for aye forgot.

But though that British army range

Each midnight on that journey strange,
No eye can see their forms, no ear
Their footfall or their voices hear,
Save on one night—upon that night
When dies away the waning light
Of the last moon of all the year :
Then if thou stand by Grisedale mere,
Betwixt the midnight hour and dawn,
When spirits move and graveyards yawn,
Through Grisedale Hause to Grisedale tide
Thou'lt see a ghostly army glide
In Keltic harness—such a host
Fought the first Roman on our coast.
See thou provoke them not to strife,
'Twere likeliest to cost thy life.
But should'st thou venture to accost
By Father, Son, and Holy Ghost,
And bid them show thee where the crown
In Grisedale mere lies low a-down,
They needs must show thee ; and if then
Thou take the crown, they ne'er again
Shall leave their grave for Grisedale tarn,
Nor Dunmail ever leave his cairn ;
But other king shall free the land
From Saxon, Dane, and Norman hand.
So, if thou see that spirit host,
In pity do not thou accost,
Nor to indulge an idle whim

Or caitiff greed do harm to him ;
But gaze with awe and tell the tale
Of that weird army of Dunmail.

Kit said, " Professor you can tell
A good ghost story very well :
But is it true?"   He shook his head.
" I would not vouch it.   Dunmail's dead,
If e'er he lived, and no one sights
His host on any other nights.
I can't say more : the legend's old,
And on the Cumbrian mountains told
Close by the cairn.   Your course is clear,
If you want more, to take ship there,
And on the trysting night camp out
On Mount Helvellyn.   It's about
As cold a place and cold a time
As any in the English clime."
Kit laughed back that she'd " take his word,
And treat as gospel all she heard,"
And fearing Phil, and sparing Lil
Her dear Professor, challenged Will
To billiards, while the scouted one
Fell back upon Maud Morrison,
To dance his disappointment off,
Impatient as a Romanoff
At being crossed, no better pleased
Because his friends had often teased
Will as a lover undeclared.
Far better the Professor fared,
He had plain sailing, no one shared

His fancy.   All were blinded by
The brighter light that was so nigh.
These nights were golden nights for Lil,
She thought she ne'er could have her fill
Of the bright stream of wit and lore
Which from his honied lips did pour.
He seemed to have lived everywhere,
And to know all things great and fair.
Then he was manly, and he seemed
Like one who, while he did much, dreamed
Of higher spheres for him in store.
Lil oft had been in love before,
But not for men with hopes sublime
Of leaving their impress on time.
    And he, what did he think of her ?
A ray of light, a soft zephyr,
A fair wild flower not too bright
Or large for love, an exquisite
And simple air reminding him
Of ballads sung in twilight dim
By Tweedside, the Breton Ysolde,
Or Enid of the legend old.

Eight o'clock saw them all arrive
In harness for a rabbit drive,
At the front door, then breakfast o'er
And luncheon packed and to the fore,
Kit with her feet in cowhide laced,
And with her Norfolk jacket's waist
Encircled with a cartridge belt,
And with a slouched man's hat of felt
Pressed down upon her golden hair,
As though quite ignorant how fair,
Was the face hidden underneath.
    Hall had besought that Lachlan Smith
Should somehow be refused a gun,
If only in apparent fun,
After his feats of yesterday.
And Will descried an easy way
By screwing both the nipples out
From his gunlock to save all doubt,
Which Smith did not discover till
He fired both barrels and heard—nil.
Of course all present sympathised,
And search-parties were organised
To find the nipples (safe and sound
In Will's watch-pocket, so not found).
Will to crown everything explained,
That now no other gun remained,

So that, unless they were found out,
Lachlan perforce must go without.
This left seven guns, for Chesterfield
Liked in a modest way to wield
His central fire, and Kit could kill
Almost as certainly as Will,
And Mr Forte came out to-day.
  The shooting, some ten miles away,
On broken 'stony rises' lay,
And as the rabbits were so thick
That one could kill them with a stick
Not seldom, stores of cartridges
Were half the battle, and horses
Were wanted for the men to ride
As 'stops' to head the rabbit-tide
Which poured before the guns in flood.
So no one of the party rode.
But Will and Albert Hall and Kit,
Left over from the waggonette
And buggy, took their quarters up
In a spring-waggon full to top
With ammunition, guns, and lunch,
And fodder for the nags to munch.
Kit drove because her favourite grey
Was needed for the shafts to-day,
Will by her ready to assist
In case its mettle tried her wrist,
And Hall in futile search for ease
Among the guns and cartridges.
Phil drove the buggy, Margaret
Being his partner, Maud not yet

Having forgiven the neglect
He'd offered to her self-respect,
And Mr Forte the waggonette,
With Lil and the Professor set
Upon the box-seat, Lil was tasked
To do just what she would have asked,
If she had ventured to, to ride
Her father and his guest beside.
    Arrived, the ladies took their seat
Beneath some rocks to 'scape the heat,
First looking round to see that they
Had no snake-neighbour in the way,
While Kit and all the gentlemen
Were starting off on their campaign
With horsemen on their left and right
And horsemen in the front to fright
The rabbits back, who broke away.
Kit fired the first shot of the day,
A true one—followed in a breath
By all except poor Lachlan Smith
Who first discovered his ill-luck
When on void blocks his hammers struck.
There is not much variety
In shooting rabbits where they lie
As thick as negroes in the hold
Of a slave-schooner used of old.
The chief of the excitement lay
In watching columns break away
In desperation, closely packed,
Between the horsemen though they cracked
Their stock-whips loud as musket-shots,

And covered all the likely spots,
Or when a serpent's angry hiss
Caused some one in a start to miss
Only to turn upon his foe
And end him with a shot or blow.
Serpents were too abundant far,
As on the 'Rises' oft they are,
Mostly not large but venomous.
One of them was so curious
(Quite six feet long and rather thin,
With bright canary-coloured skin),
That Mr Forte when it was dead,
Fixing it just behind the head,
In cleft-stick, gave it to a man
To carry back to the spring-van,
Meaning to send it up to town
To the museum.   'Black' and 'Brown'
'Tiger' and 'whip' and 'copperhead'
'Carpet' and 'Diamond,' the dread
'Death-Adder's' self he'd chanced to spy
In some part of the colony
At one time or another—none
Of the same colour as this one.
   A battue in an English wood
Of pheasants trained to take their food
From Keeper's hands has less excuse
Than rabbit-drives, which have their use.
For rabbits are as dire a foe
As the wolves stamped out long ago,
And battues are as merciful
As arsenic or traps which pull

Their limbs off but don't kill outright.
　A rabbit drive presents a sight
Which those who in the dear old land
Shoot only, scarce can understand.
When once the line begins to drive
The ground seems verily alive
And one incessant roar of guns
Tells how the tale of slaughter runs.
Now your gunbarrel follows fast
A rabbit as in frantic haste
Along the jutting rocks he flies
Which bound and break the distant rise,
And now you hunch your back to bring
Your fire upon them as they spring
Right at your feet, now wheel sharp round
On one which short reprieve had found
By lying close till you had passed
Now right, now left, until at last
Your cartridges away you've shot
Or find your barrels grown too hot
To hold with comfort.　You let lie
Your rabbits just where they may die.
No one would for a minute stop
To pick the mangled vermin up
But leave them for the hawks and 'cats'
And ants that haunt their habitats,—
So vast a difference it makes
When the supply demand o'ertakes.
　Luncheon suggested, none demurred
But hailed it as a welcome word.
The sun was hot, the ground was rough

The tussocks plentiful and tough,
And they had had three hours or more
Of walking without rest.   Will bore
The palm for shooting.   Chesterfield
Least deftly did his weapon wield.
Kit was astonished much to see
How steadily and sturdily
Cobham strode on (But Will told her
That as a rule the English were
Great walkers—better walkers far
Than average Australians are),
And what fine shots he sometimes made
Though he missed often.   She displayed
Some skill herself and Mr Forte
Still shot well and enjoyed the sport.
    At lunch the shooters quenched their thirst
With various liquors.   Beer was first
In favour, claret next.   But Will
And Mr Forte prepared to fill
With oatmeal-water, which they said
Was the best drink for health and head
When one was hot.   While Phil endured
Water with only whiskey cured.
    Lunch over, the Professor went
To chat with Lil, with whom he spent
The smoking hour, soon joined by Kit,
Who feared an amatory fit
From Phil and sought to give redress
For her enforced obtrusiveness
By telling Lil how good a shot
And how enduring and what not

Her friend had proved, while Phil blew forth
In gusty puffs of smoke his wrath.

     *   *   *   *

That night two fresh deserters joined
The two who had at first declined,
The lawyer and Maud Morrison,
Maud, maybe, if the truth were known,
For Phil, and Lachlan Smith for her.
Success was with the barrister.
For Phil and Hall had sauntered out
To-night again to smoke about.

    Ida's suggestion, that three men,
Before the ladies chose again
Should choose a subject, pleasing most
Will was selected for the post,
Who for the evening's story chose
Life in an English manor-house.

    When he some minutes had delayed
To ponder, the Professor said
The tale is one I heard at home
From Fred Rowe, my old college chum.
So he shall tell you, word for word
Where I remember, what I heard.

ETHEL.

Katie is a pretty shrew ;
Isabel a little blue ;
Maud as proud as Lucifer ;
Christobel a sonneteer ;

Edith is reserv'd and fair ;
Eleanor hath auburn hair ;
Margaret is masculine ;
I don't care for Adeline ;
Beatrix is very sweet ;
And hath many at her feet ;
Nothing hath she ever harm'd,
But an iceberg's sooner warmed ;
She's so dully temperate
That she cannot even hate ;
All her useful life is spent
In the tedious content
That in story-books befalls
Angels and good animals.
Mary is a peacemaker,
All the people round love her,
And I love her passively,
But she is too good for me.
Daring Ethel is a queen,
Most majestic in her mien
And most royal in her ways ;
All the men her beauty praise,
Not before her royal face
If they dread condign disgrace.
Admiration in your eyes
Is her look'd-for, lawful prize ;
Admiration in your speech
Is a statutable breach

Of Her Grace's social code.
No one ever waltz'd or rode,
Shot an arrow or a glance,
With more finish'd elegance ;
Neither is she over-bold,
Callous, feelingless, nor cold.
If she sees a rough young squire
Reeling backwards from the fire
Of a merciless coquette
For his uncouth etiquette,
She will cross a crowded room
To alleviate his doom,
Make him come and sit by her,
Be a smiling listener
To the 'bag' of yesterday,
Where the warmest corners lay
In the Earl of Foxshire's woods :
How his blood-mare swam the floods,
Of the row with Farmer Scroggs,
And the names of all the dogs.
And if talk-about is true
Ethel can be tender too.
Who remembers Dick Duval,
Once the favourite of all ?
Honest, hearty, handsome Dick,
Brave, and generous, and quick,
But there was no runagate
Ever so unfortunate.

Dicky never could escape,
As a schoolboy, from a scrape;
Dick was never in a brawl
But he came off worst of all;
He, whose share was often least,
Bore the blame of all the rest.
Dick at last—it ne'er appear'd
Why or wherefore—was cashier'd,
Driven from his father's hall,
Scowl'd upon and shunn'd by all.
Dick to queenly Ethel came:
Ethel had no word of blame,
Did not turn away or frown,
Ask'd no explanation,
Wrung his slack hand heartily,
And, looking at him earnestly,
In a sweet firm whisper said:
"I can trust you, Dick; you did
Nothing base, or mean, or low;
What you did I do not know.
Do not tell me—only say
That you would not turn away
From a man who did the same
As from one whose touch was shame."
While a tear splash'd in the dust,
"Bless you, Ethel, for your trust,"
Was the broken-voic'd reply;
"Never such a thing did I.

But I came to say good-bye :
I am going to the East,
Under Osman to enlist,
From my name to wipe the stain,
And retrieve fair fame again."
" Dick, I will not bid you stay,
Go and wipe the stain away ;
One thing promise me, that you
Nothing in despair will do ;
Try to come safe home again,
You have one who will remain
E'er your firm and faithful friend ;
Promise, Dick, and try to mend,
No more getting into scrapes,
No more hazardous escapes,
Saving when you face the foe,
But then do as brave men do ;
Wait until the battle—then
Give your gallant heart the rein ;
And, if you have time to write,
Send the story of a fight
Bravely fought and bravely won,
How you are, and what you've done ;
Saying when, your penance o'er,
You are coming home once more,
And where letters will reach you."
" Who will write them, if I do ? "
" I myself, Dick." " You will ? " " Yes,

I do not desert distress."
"And can you, who are so fair,
Coveted by all men, care—
Stoop to correspond with me?"
"Correspond? Yes, certainly.
Dick I place you far before
All the faultless fools who bore
One to death with etiquette;
Who have nothing to regret,
Not because no ill they've wrought,
But because they've not done aught
Saving sleep, and drink, and eat,
And I hold the manly heat
That lands you in scrape and stain
Far above the force of brain
That leads some men to apply
Lifetimes to philosophy,
In contempt of common things—
Births, and loves, and buryings.
You've been hearty to excess,
But I like you none the less."
"Hear me, Ethel, I am mad,
But I am not wholly bad;
I am mad, but going away
For long months, perhaps for aye;
Hear me, Ethel, long have I
Loved you most devotedly,
In the days when I was heir

To the acres broad and fair
Which are mine no longer now,
In the bright days of my youth
And wild days of later growth.
But you ever seem'd too good,
Of too queenly womanhood,
And too wonderful to be
For a simple man like me.
Hear me, Ethel, ere I go,—
Hear me,—I would have you know
That I love you as none can
But a passion-ridden man.
Hear me; if I live to come,
With refurbish'd honour, home,
And you e'er should need my aid,
If in life-blood it were paid,
I would shed it every drop
To give you a minute's hope.
But if I should never come,
Try to clear my name at home.
I will write you all the tale
Of this last scrape while I sail.
Good-bye, Ethel: do you weep?
Tears for worthier sorrows keep;
I'm not worth a single tear
From your lashes.   Ethel dear,
Darling Ethel, do not cry."
"Wait, Dick, do not say good-bye,

I love you too : if you still
Wish to marry me, I will
Wish to marry you, love." "No,
Not when I have sunk so low ;
You who seemed too good for me
In my old prosperity.
Darling, you would stoop too far,
Fair and noble as you are.
I am, do I what I can,
A dishonourable man."
"Not dishonourable, Dick ;
Ills have fallen fast and thick
On your wild, unlucky head,
But I know you truly said
You've not done since you were born
What would make you shrink in scorn
From a man who'd done the same,
As from one whose touch was shame.
Dick, you shall not leave me thus."
"You are over-generous."
"If I may not be your wife
I'll be single all my life ;
But I will not bid you stay
Till the stain is wip'd away
By good service bravely done
On the field of action ;
But when you come home again
I'll be yours if you are fain."

Dick look'd at her wistfully.
" Ethel, is this charity—
Just your nobleness of heart,
Seeing all my friends depart
But yourself—or is it true?"
" True : I always have loved you ;
But if you had come to me
In your wild prosperity
Then I should have answer'd, No,
Not until you've learn'd to show
What good stuff you're moulded of.
When you've proven this, enough,
I will gladly be your wife.
But while all you do is rife
With outrage and escapade,
I would sooner be a maid.
Now, you do not need advice,
But the light of loving eyes."

" Sweet, this generosity
Too heroic is for me ;
I can't be so generous
As to once again refuse
Such a crown of love as this.
Darling Ethel, let me kiss
Your kind hand before I go."
" Let you kiss my hand, Dick ! No :
Kiss my lips ; they're not too good

For a brave man : spare your blood
And spare life whene'er you may,
Strike home on a doubtful day ;
If you can write to me, try ;
Good-bye, dear old Dick, good-bye ! "

This is Ethel's mystery,
No one knows it all but me.
Ethel bearded Squire Duval
In his study at the hall,
Told him Dick was not to blame,
But his answer was the same.
" Dick's disgraced an ancient line,
He's no longer son of mine."
But there's nought he will not do,
If Queen Ethel asks him to,
Saving this ; and on a day,
After Ethel's gone away,
He will say, with almost joy,
" She did not desert my boy."

When you look upon her face,
In her beauty you can trace
Something wistful now and then ;
Then she turns and smiles again
On her waiting worshippers :
They know not this spur of hers
Press'd against her noble heart,

And, when bootless they depart,
Mutter slanders of coquette.
I myself should not know yet
Were it not that Dick and I
Were school-cronies formerly,
Shared a study and a crib,
Had a fight : I broke his rib,
He made music in my head.
When he went away, he said :
" Ethel, I've told all to Fred ;
He and I are limb and limb,
Make a confidant of him
When you want to talk of me."
This is how I came to be
Privy to her sacrifice.
Often, with her grave sweet eyes,
Fasten'd on me, she will ask
Me of every trick and task
Of his scapegoat schoolboy life.
He is worthy such a wife ;
Try your best, you will not find
Better fellow of his kind.
He'd have been a famous knight
In the bright enchanted night
Of Provençal chivalry.
Modern-times reality,
Like a dull unwelcome day,
Drove the magic night away

With its legendary grace.
When I look upon her face,
Making Dick a schoolboy Cid,
Rubbing up the feats he did,
And her grateful fluent eyes
Give me eloquent replies,
Oft I wish that I might plead
Someone else's cause instead.

But I have a pet as well,
Lovely, laughing, light-heart Nell.
We don't talk of love, but play
At it all and every day:
I steal kisses and she laughs,
Swear they're earnest, and she chaffs.
Once, when I contrived to go
Underneath the misletoe,
Saying she'd a score to pay,
She kiss'd me and tripp'd away,
Not too quickly to be caught,
And with well-feign'd struggles brought
Underneath the bough once more.
We've had quarrels o'er and o'er,
But we always make it up,
Neither cares to sulk or mope.
    If my sisters hint that I
Feel for Nellie tenderly,
I'm indignant, and retort,

From a well-assur'd report,
Of Sir This, and Captain That,
Giving tits for every tat.
  If her cousin, Bertie Bell,
Whispers spitefully to Nell,
" Nellie, you're in love with Fred,"
She will toss her pretty head,
And, with mock humility,
Drop a curtsey and reply,
" Well, and if your charge were true,
Better far with Fred than you."
All the same one's fidgety
When the other is not by.
We engage at ev'ry ball
For the waltzes one and all :
Waltzing's too divine a dance
To be left to common chance :
You should only waltz with one
In such perfect unison
With you, as you cannot get
Save you often practise it :
Squares we always give away.
When it's supper time, we stay
Till the extras all are done,
Then we go and sup alone,
Make the mottoes vehicles
For the truths one never tells
Without such occasion.

Whispering we linger on
Until we away are sent
Or slip into sentiment :
Then we go and waltz again
Feeling fire in ev'ry vein :
Nellie shuts a blithe blue eye
In delicious ecstasy,
As we float (we hate to haste),
And I clasp her slender waist
With a more expressive arm :
Sweet abandon is her charm :
Nellie looks her loveliest
When the sunny elf-locks, press'd
In the heavy plaits behind,
Play the truant in the wind,
And the errand-blushes stay
And don't hurry straight away
Soon as they have said their say.

Ev'ry Christmas here we meet
At my father's country seat,
Staying for a month or more :
Ev'ry Christmas, when it's o'er,
Many wish it would begin
And think breaking-up a sin.
Nell and I are worst of all,
We'd like Christmas day to fall
Once a month : and now I find

That I must make up my mind;
For we clearly can't go on
In the way we've always done;
Nellie will be eighteen soon,
I was twenty-one in June.

'Twas windy, and so when he ceased
All hasted in, Kit first, ill-pleased
At the unconquered Ethel's fall
Which seemed almost prophetical.
  I would have said all went but Lil,
Who braved discomfort and the chill,
To steal a tête-à-tête, and said,
" Is Ethel Kit?"   He shook his head.
" For many reasons, no.   Firstly,
'Twould be gross personality;
And secondly, while Ethel loved
Her beauty's due, Miss Johnstone's moved
By no such female weaknesses;
And thirdly, she affects the dress
Of gentlemen and manly sports,
While Ethel's foibles and fortes
Were feminine.   No Amazon
Professed was she, but merely one
Of those proud high-bred English dames
Of families with ancient names
And great estates, who scorn to stoop
In marriage, but whose eyes look up
To some high union which time
Has in his hand for them, sublime

In their ambitions.   They are right;
Why should a girl, at first invite,
Haste to throw heart and hand away,
The one trump-card she has to play?"
"But who was Nellie?   Are all girls
Who don't aspire to dukes and earls
And premiers and millionaires
So easy in their love affairs
As Nell!" asked Lil, who thought, if so,
That her wings were a little slow,
And England certainly must be
A country of the brave and free,
And recollecting how she had,
While they were still a child and lad,
Enjoyed a romp of kiss and pet
With Ted, Kit's brother, fancied yet
That if such romps were etiquette
They might sometimes be very nice.
He answered with this sage advice
For one in the near neighbourhood
Of a fair girl with southern blood
And rosy lips and yielding mien,
That "Nells could not be often seen
Even in England, where Mammas
And Mrs Grundy and papas
Shut off the naughty and the nice
From girls with barriers of ice,
That romps at home as well as school
Were the exception not the rule,
But there were boys who would be boys
And girls who looked for other joys .

Than church and fancy work and tea,
That Nells there were and needs must be
In every age, in every clime,
As long as there is space or time,
Nells who rejoice to cull the flower
Which grows on every passing hour."
And then he pulled her on his knee
And kissed her, asking her if she
Had not been treated thus before,
And, she not struggling, gave her more
And added in a whisper " Lil,
Will you?" when she replied " I will "
And put her little hands in his
And held her lips up for a kiss.

Now mark the wit of womankind,
And learn that love is not so blind
As poets picture him to be,
For when Lil sought her bedroom she,
While still the gentlemen sat to
Their glass of water—and Lochdhu,
Called in her mother and confessed,
Entreating her to do her best
To win her father to her choice,
Pleading with that sweet gentle voice
Which won all hearers to her part.
Now Helen had a tender heart,
And her ten yearning years of troth
Tended to make her very loath
Her children's longings to postpone
A single month: and Lil was one

To give her much anxiety.
She was so pretty and so free
From guile as well as self-restraint,
And he would have to be a saint
Who scorned her gentle glowing charms
And shrank from her extended arms.
  She had been wooed three times before,
And each' time thrown the wooer o'er
With much reluctance—souls of make
Like hers love Love for its own sake.
Her other lovers had been men
As much drawn by the hope of gain
In marrying the squatter's child
As by the face which on them smiled ;
But the Professor had a clear
Six or eight hundred pounds a year
Of salary, e'en suppose he had
No penny of his own to add,
A sum with which as bachelor
He certainly could do much more,
Than married with as much again.
That he was capable was plain
From his appointment : and his mind
Seemed honourable, broad, and kind :
He was nice-looking in the face,
And gentlemanly in his ways,
And 'Chesterfield' had said that he
Came of a good old family.
Then Lily seemed so fond of him,
And, if it was no passing whim
But an absorbing love . . . . (and she

Owned to a sensibility
Herself of the Professor's charm).
Nor was Lil kept in long alarm,
For, when her father came to bed,
The mother for the daughter pled
So winningly that his consent
Was granted her incontinent,
Subject to conversation due
Upon the morrow with the two.
Kind Helen, far too kind to keep
A darling daughter from her sleep
With doubt and trembling on a theme
So near her heart as this would seem,
Stole to her bedroom on tip-toe,
Her prayer's success to let her know.

  *   *   *   *

But reader, be it not supposed
That Lil and her Professor closed
Their interesting interview
So very briefly as I do.
Whatever at the time had been
Her satisfaction at fourteen
When Ted had petted her, she now
Felt to herself inclined to vow
That it was not a patch upon
That which she just had undergone,
And was prepared to undergo
Till further notice—in the glow
Of mutual love oblivious quite
Of the chill roughness of the night,
Which maybe, since it kept the rest

Within the house, was for the best.
Here Lil disclosed confidingly
(Still nestling on her lover's knee,
While her soft damask cheeks and lips
Frequently underwent eclipse),
What palpitations of dismay
The story of Nausicaa
Had wakened, how she'd nursed a dread
That he would turn out to be wed,
Though it did not at first occur
What difference it made to her;
How she had shuddered at the day
When he would have to go away,
Although he, it was obvious,
Could not be always at their house;
That truly she had never thought
Of marriage with him, but had sought
His company because she found
That days went far more blithely round
In his society, than when
She talked with ordinary men."
He said, when in due time his lips
Could spare the leisure from their sips,
"Your parents may think my demand
And your surrender of your hand
A trifle premature upon
A four days' introduction.
But four days are enough to show
How pleasantly my life will go
With you as help-mate, and you seem
To know enough of me, to deem

That I shall fairly well fulfil
What you meant when you said 'I will.'
A stranger in a far-off land
Drifts till he finds a friendly strand
In some fair, gentle girl like you
To moor his wandering bark unto.
Had I the loneliness but known
Of living in strange lands alone,
I should have wedded ere I left
Rather than face it out, bereft
Of father's, brother's, sister's face,
Without a wife's to take their place.
This is my answer to the world.
If it with lip and nostril curled
Hints that my suit was rather short,
Your father's sanction I shall court
With the fair rank I hold in life
And proof that I can give a wife
A decent, comfortable home,
Though small enough to you who come
From one like this.   My plea to you
Is that you represent my view
Of gentle, graceful womanhood,
Neither too clever nor too good,
To be caressing when one's tired
And like being petted and admired,
Intelligent enough to take
An interest in plans I make
And what I write and what I do
But not what Frenchmen call 'a blue.'
Women of genius and those

Who would their own impress impose
On everything a husband does
Should chose a husband like the wife
Whom I invite to share my life
Contented to appreciate,
And seeking not to mould, their fate.
There cannot in one household be
Two-in-command and harmony.
  I have been candid with you, Lil,
And told you how you so fulfil
My beau-ideal of a wife.
You have the merry pride of life,
The beauty that allures the eye
The grace of form and gait, the shy
But never-failing sympathy,
The easy, gracious courtesy,
And tender girlish helplessness,
And more that I can ill express. "

December 29th—Sunday.

Two persons we may feel quite sure
Found that the morning air was pure,
And wondered why folks slept away
The nicest two hours in the day,
Lil and her lover.   Lil was drest,
As suited the occasion best,
In the same gossamery white
Which first on Christmas-day saw light.
The morn was young and so was she
And both were fresh as fresh can be :
'Twas early summer in the year
And early summer too in her,
And nothing looks so apposite
To early summer as pure white.
　　He picked some fresh forget-me-not
For her to wreath about her throat
And now, as then, her slender waist
With a broad pale blue sash was laced.
　　Unless to scepticism slave,
Behold an instance of brain-wave.
For ere their blithe good-night they bade
No word had Lil or Cobham said
Of early rising.   Yet they both,
Though as a rule extremely loath
To quit their bed's society,
Were up in time to see the sky

Grey with the promise of the dawn
And the dew sparkling on the lawn,
Each speculating on the chance
Of a praeprandial romance.
   Had she been roguishly inclined
She might have tried her lover's mind
Being 'en rapport' of the plot
And how t' would end, which he was not.
But Lil was open as the day
And rushed to him with glad "we may,"
As soon as they were face to face
Lending herself to his embrace,
With some soft blushes as protest,
And toss of her dishevelled crest
When it was over. "Yes, we may,"
Repeated she, nor drew away
Her waist from his endearing arm,
But yielded to the subtle charm,
Which gentle women oft confess,
Of feeling her own helplessness.
"Last night, when we good-night had said,
Before my father came to bed,
I called my mother and disclosed
The solemn fact that you'd proposed
And I'd accepted wedded bliss,
Subject to her consent and his,
And begged the question of her own
By confidently going on
And asking her to intercede
With Father and my cause to plead.
Which she so eloquently did

That he consented, subject to
A satisfactory talk with you.
And—was not dear old mother kind?—
She stole to me to ease my mind
With the good news before she turned
T' enjoy the sleep she'd so well earned.
  " Father would like it, if you'd walk
With him to church, to have the talk.
He says that both of you will be
Just twice as easy and as free,
If you are in the open air,
As cooped up in his study there,
And that the motion will inspire
Your words with swing if not with fire.
I'm sure he will not be severe,
But if he is, be patient dear,
And talk him over—as you can
If you are as expert with man."

  The upshot of the walk was this
That the dull sermon seemed like bliss
To the Professor, for he sate
To Lily most approximate
And whispered to her a kill-care
Before he breath'd his bidding pray'r.
And when the ' voluntary' rose
From the harmonium to close
The service, kindly Mr Forte
Asked—sotto voce—if Lil thought
The walk would be too much for her
(To rest him since he had walked there

Was the excuse, although he went
Backwards and forwards quite content
On ev'ry Sunday of the year),
And when the waggonette was clear
Of greeting neighbours, he turned round
And told what fairly might astound
Miss Ridley, Madge, and Chesterfield,
And Maud and Ida, who appealed
For abnegation of the tale
To Mrs Forte without avail.
 That Lil with Cobham walked alone
Had indeed struck Maud Morrison,
As rather odd, considering
What kind folks say of such a thing,
Nor could she the engagement eye
Without some pangs of jealousy,
Not that she envied Lil her lover
(She'd have refused him three times over
Had he addressed his suit to her),
But in that Lil without demur
The object of her choice had gained
And every consent obtained.
 Maud was a pretty butterfly
Whom all admired as she flew by
But every man forbore to touch
Lest she should crumble in his clutch.
Besides to marry a poor belle,
Who hopes to dress and drive out well,
Need a long purse, and Midases
Are fond of bachelorial ease.
 Ida was filled with pure delight,

As she was ever, at the sight
Of fresh-begotten happiness.
Madge was too shy her thoughts t' express
But a soft radiance filled the skies
Of her magnificent blue eyes.
Like Maud, Miss Ridley felt a pang
From jealousy's envenomed fang
That true love's course should be so smooth
To some folks in their earliest youth,
While others had to wait and wait,
Poor suppliants at the feet of fate.
She'd had a lover of her own
Since dear old girlish days byegone,
And that suggestive word ' Engage '
Recalled a towered parsonage
(Towered against the reiving hand
Of Scotsmen) in Northumberland,
Where a shy curate tried to tell
The tale which Lil had liked so well.

But soon the paroxysm passed
Before a joy that was to last,
That her pet pupil, whom she loved
More than her own kin, thus was moved
By one whom everyone approved.
And Chesterfield, a bachelor
Of forty-three or forty-four,
Seized the occasion to descant
On the advantages which haunt
An early marriage, and went on
In his own pleasing way to con
All the Professor's pleasing traits

And say the utmost in his praise.
  One good result did really come
Of these two lovers walking home,
That those, who had not been to church,
Were not left blindly in the lurch
But posted in the present state
Of matters, ere they reached the gate.
And doubtless they enjoyed the treat
Of trudging through the dust and heat
More than a comfortable seat
In the paternal waggonette
Where seven other persons met.
  Dinner on Sunday being at two
Arose the question what to do
In the whole hour, which intervened
'Twixt front door reached and soup tureened,
Decided by a hint from Will
That there might be some ' cats ' to kill,
Who, hearing the Professor vent
Expressions of astonishment,
Said that the victim slaughtered thus
Was not the old domestic puss
But native cat of ferret shape
Which would not let one fowl escape,
If it were left at liberty
To ravage and to multiply.
The trap in which the cats were snared
Was a large wooden box prepared
With inward sloping sides and lid
Pierced with a drop, secured and hid
With a long tunnel-fashioned top,

K

Baited with meat above the drop.
Will lifted off the lid and showed
Three slender, sharp-nosed creatures, cowed
And crouching to conceal themselves
Under the overhanging shelves,
And went to fetch his terriers.

But when he'd seen their spotted furs
Lil gave her lover's arm a pull ;
She was too soft and pitiful
To witness even beasts of prey
Being baited :   Nor would Cobham stay
Although he would have liked no doubt
To see the rivals fight it out,
As cat and dog proverbially
Do when they meet in enmity.

Two cats they coursed, of which the one
Was caught and killed ere he had run
A dozen yards, the other, given
A longer start to make things even,
Escaped into a firewood-stack.
A 'pup' was then put in t' attack
The third, a staunch fox-terrier
Who did not show one sign of fear,
Though he had not before this one
Been set to face a 'cat' alone,
But boldly grappled with his foe
And would not whine or let it go,
Although it made its sharp teeth meet
Right through the skin of his forefeet.

Near sundown in the afternoon
They took the terriers for a run

About the paddocks,—I should say
All but the two betrothed, for they
Wiled the delicious hours away
Upon a rustic garden seat
Secured from passing gaze and heat
By a huge Wellingtonia's boughs
Sloped downwards—a live summerhouse,
With branches six feet from the ground
Inside, and on the turf all round.
The others sat down while the dogs
Hunted or scratched at hollow logs
And holes beneath the gum-tree roots
For 'possums,' 'cats,' and bandicoots,
And here and there a rabbit who
Had not had time to get into
His proper burrow.   Once they were
Attracted to a terrier
Whose hind paws only could be seen
His body being hidden in
A fallen tree, whence after close
And lengthy struggle, by the nose
He drew an old buck 'possum' out
Instantly set on by the rout
And torn to pieces.—To resist
Impossible.—And once there hissed
An angry serpent from a log
Stirred by a stick because no dog
Would enter to drag out again
A rabbit which had refuge ta'en.

    *   *   *   *

All vied in kindliness to Lil

Her cup of ectasy to fill
To overflowing. She had been
So warm and gentle in her mien
To everyone. The only chaff,
Tempered by a disarming laugh,
Was Kit's, who put it in this wise
" It's not fair to monopolize
The only safe man of them all
Who may not, if he wants to, fall
In love with us, with whom we can
Enjoy ourselves like man with man,
Without inspiring false alarms
Of being victims to their charms.
  " Lil, you our benefactress are
For thus disabling for the war
Another of the skirmishers
Hovering to cut off stragglers
Who chance to fall out from the flanks
Of the firm Amazonian ranks.
  " A woman can't be fair and free
Without men fancying that she
Acknowledges their kindling eye
And irresistibility."
          *   *   *   *

There was no story told that night,
Not because Lil's new found delight
Demanded leisure undisturbed,
For 'twould have any how been curbed
By Mr Forte's religiousness.
He did not his religion press
At point of bayonet down one's throat

And did not quit his path to note
Irregularities, which he,
Walking straight forward, would not see.
But when it came to yes or no
He never doubted what to do.
He was a man who served his Lord
In deed, in thought, in will, in word,
But held that ' practice' and not 'preach'
Was the true Christian way to teach.

Before they went to bed, they'd made
Arrangements for a fusillade
Of waterfowl upon a lake
Some six miles off and, for Lil's sake,
Will had proposed that she should ride
With the Professor by her side,
Saying that he would bring a gun
For him and bidding them ride on
Because the ' trap ' would overtake
The riders ere they reached the lake,
But if they reached it first to wait
Below the hill-crest at the gate
So that the ducks might not be scared
Before the ambush was prepared.

   *   *   *   *

The dam was of a crescent shape
With broad lagoons at either cape :
But in the middle just a thread
Of water filmed its muddy bed :
And here the angle of a fence
Gave a slight line of cover, whence
An ambushed gun might be close to
The mobs of ducks and swans which flew
In terror towards the top lagoon
When started from the lower one.
And here Will posted Phil and Hall

As really the best post of all,
Although he thought that visitors
Were likely to prefer the course
Which he himself proposed to take
Of stalking first the lower lake
And then the upper, where they could
See all the wildfowl-brotherhood
Wading or floating on the mere
And starting up as they drew near.
   Will had arranged that Kit should go
With Phil and Hall knowing that so
She would have better sport, which she
Loved fully as devotedly
As any gaitered gentleman
Upon the Twelfth of August can.
But she refused to, from a fear
That Phil might prove sole cavalier.
   The party, who were left to stalk,
After a minute's stealthy walk
Over the low ridge of a hill,
Burst on a spectacle to fill
The least enthusiastic mind
With rapture.   The whole dam was lined
With teal and divers, geese and swans
And avocets and pelicans,
With ducks of half the species known
To colonists, ' musk ' ' black ' and ' brown,'
Wood-ducks and mountain-ducks galore,
Blue-wings and full a dozen more,
With gulls and plovers on the shore
And snippets at the water-edge,

And bitterns rising from the sedge.
As soon as they had topped the crest
A swan, the sentry for the rest,
Gave the alarm with one long note,
Which still was ringing in his throat,
When swish in one immense efflux
Arose innumerable ducks
Leaving just stray ones here and there
For the gun-barrels brought to bear
With instant swiftness on the spot,
Where they had swam, with hail of shot.
Kit bagged a brace of black-duck, Will
Who hardly ever failed to kill
A leash, and the Professor, who
Missed with his first, with number two
Brought down a swan so far that it
Seemed quite impossible to Kit,
While Chesterfield had the good-luck
To find a diplomatic duck,
Who'd rather take its chance and stay
Among the reeds than fly away.
   But Phil and Hall, as Will had said,
Enjoyed best sport, for overhead,
Soon as the stalkers came in sight
Of one lagoon, arose a flight,
As thick as locusts, of huge flocks
Of swans and geese and teal and ducks,
One after other, steering for
The far lagoon's remotest shore,
Scarce noticing the ambush laid
Beneath the fence's treacherous shade.

Both were good shots and, when the last
Of the migrating 'mobs' had passed,
Some dozen dying birds and dead
Lay on the ground or with sunk head
Floated upon the shallow pool
Which linked the two lagoons—so cool
And calculating was the aim
With which they timed the passing game.
　The stalkers, 'sneaking' round to try
The far lake, found the ducks more shy
And only shot a brace or two
Of plover, while but few 'mobs' flew
Over the ambush and those few
So high as to be out of range.
　Then Will suggested as a change
(Because the ducks would be too wild
To be again that day beguiled,
And more were lying dead than could
Be eaten while their flesh kept good)
That they should drive across and kill
The rabbits swarming on the hill.
　But Lil and the Professor found
Following plover round and round
(She on her horse and he on foot
In case he had a chance to shoot)
More to their taste ; nor did he find
That he lost sport to stay behind,
For several plover and a crane
Soon fell, and once Lil drew her rein
And pointed to a patch of grey
Down by the water far away,

And bade him draw his cartridges,
And put in 'eights' instead of 'threes,'
And steal up to the snippet cloud
And fire both barrels and reload,
In case a bittern should be scared
Out of the reeds.   He thus prepared,
Two dozen 'pipers' bleeding lay
Upon the sand, an easy prey,
And, loading fast and aiming well,
A huge, soft, mottled bittern fell
Which rose up from the sedge as soon
As the shot rang o'er the lagoon.
He tried to stalk a pelican
But ever since the sentry swan
Had uttered his first warning note,
They had not ventured within shot
Or even sight.   And half the while
He hung upon Lil's radiant smile
And fresh voice so attentively
That many a wary duck flew by
Unnoticed until out of reach,
While he was making some sweet speech.
    Will, as he drove away, had cried
That if they piled the game beside
The fence 'neath which the ambush lay
He would drive back again that way
And bring it home—of course in jest,
Not dreaming that the sporting zest
Of the Professor would suffice
Even one minute to entice
His eyes from Lil's, when they were once

Hidden behind a friendly sconce,
And giving it no second thought,
Though it was piled up to brought,
For Lil had seen enough to tell
How untrained horses hate the smell
Of wild game, but did not perceive
That Will was laughing in his sleeve.
  However, after dinner, she
Turned the laugh on him guilelessly
By asking where the bittern was,
Which he'd brought home for them, because
They wished to have it skinned. "Bittern?"
He said not knowing where to turn
"What bittern?" "Didn't you come back
As you said, by the morning's track
To pick the game up?" "Game up? No,
You never thought I would, did you?"
"Of course we did. We hung it up,
Just where you told us, on the top
Of the two fences, where they meet,
Where Phil and Albert had their seat."
  "You see what comes of chaffing, Will,"
Observed his mother, asking Lil
What they had left, and when she heard
Their bag, remarked that she preferred
Snippets on toast to any bird
They'd shot in the whole morning's sport.
Whether it was that Mrs Forte
Was so inordinately fond
Of snippets nicely trussed and browned
Or wished mild censure to convey

To Will for Lil, is hard to say.
At any rate she was not wont
Her likes and dislikes to recount
At other times so forcibly.
    He only smiled, but by and by
Went out and caught a horse, and drove
The buggy to their treasure-trove,
Which, just as they were off to bed,
He brought back with diminished head
Minus the bittern, which a 'cat'
Had nibbled or a crow pecked at
Till it could scarce be recognised
For what poor Lil had so much prized.
The tale was over long ere this,
And Lil had had—well say one kiss
In the large drawing-room, which all
Abandoned to their beck and call.
    Lil was in raptures, she had not
Deemed that her lover spoke or wrote
So manfully as he had told
The story of the stormed stronghold.
She saw that like the Ithacan
Whenever in his story ran
Mention of " battles or of ships
The whole man changed " and from his lips
Poured such a stream of burning words
That he who heard beheld the swords
Dinted and red with their fierce play
And white sails bending o'er the bay.
The three poor soldiers of West Kent,
Men of the Fiftieth Regiment,

Standing upon the river-sands
Awaiting but the staff commands
To enter the Urumea,
The struggle in the riverway,
With ebbing tide and weedy rock,
And then the first tremendous shock
When they had gained the hostile banks
And down on their devoted ranks,
With not a stick of shelter nigh,
Poured the fierce hail of musketry
And canister and hand grenades,
And when, above the palisades,
They saw the glowing fire barrels
And gleaming piles of mortarshells
Upon the ramparts of the town,
And then the order to lie down
While the Trafalgar sixty-eights
Breached traverses and parapets,
And then that awful pause between
With its exploding magazine,
And then the ghastly, sickening glee
Which the survivor of the three
Showed in the storming, when he ran
His bayonet right through the man
Who'd killed his mate ; and then the·hell
Which on the conquered city fell.
    Lil as he had his tale outpoured,
Pictured him with a waving sword
Urging·his men into the breach
With manful deeds and manful speech,
And thought that he who thus could write

Would be high-hearted in the fight,
And yielded to his warm caress
With the old pleasing consciousness
Of helplessness when at his side
Deliciously intensified ;
There had been nine that night in all,
To hear the story ; Phil and Hall
Were playing billiards ; Lachlan Smith
Was marking, little pleased therewith,
And Will had driven off to find
The game which he had left behind.

The barrister, who liked to hear
The stories, had stayed out to cheer
Maud Morrison, who need expect
Little from Phil except neglect.
But so Maud thought and chose to stay
Rather than throw herself away,
As she esteemed it, upon him
If she should fail to win Phil's whim.

Chesterfield had been chosen king.
The subject of the evening
Chosen by him was history,
A battlepiece of days gone by.
Accordingly the Oxford man
In a few minutes' time began
A lay of San Sebastian,
First telling them that he designed
The pieces that were shorter-lined
As speeches of the Rank and File,
And that the longer lines meanwhile
Were narrative to tell the tale
Where speeches only needs must fail.

SAN SEBASTIAN, JULY 31st, 1813.

A LAY OF THE RANK AND FILE.

*The three
Common
Soldiers.*
We be poor men, that stand
Awaiting the command
To march with bated breath
To glory or to death ;
Nor know we well wherefore
Our rulers went to war,
Save that the name of French
Has an unwholesome stench
To the true British nose.
We can well see our foes
And all that they have done
Against our coming on.

That morning, ere the clock struck half-past ten,
Down in the British trenches all the men
Were under arms, waiting the bugle call
To sound the storming-party to the wall.
And as the tide was going down they viewed
What well might daunt the sternest hardihood,
The curtain high of solid masonry,
With bastion and hornwork and glacis,
The rampart fronting the Urumea
And sweeping with its guns the riverway,

And the retrenchments the besieged had made
With gabion, fascine, and palisade
Against surprise, or storm, or escalade.
Long-sighted men could see the bayonets
Glance in the sun behind the parapets,
And cannon with their muzzles trained to bear
Upon the breach, and piled shells, and the glare
Of fire barrels along its summit ranged.
'Twere superhuman had no colour changed
E'en in the most undaunted of them all,
And had no brave men's knees begun to fall
One on the other as they waited there.
Anxiety unmans as much as fear.
And these men had to loiter till the tide
Of the Urumea should so subside
That they might pass and press to the assault,
And ev'ry moment of this enforced halt
Saw the alert, resolute garrison
Piling up gabion on gabion,
All full of earth, and fascine on fascine,
And mounting fresh guns on the ravelin.
Time never seemed so sluggishly to move
To lover waiting for his lady love
As to these poor men, till they heard the " sound
For the advance " upon the bugle wound,
Although they knew not whether it was death
Or medalled breasts for them, and laurel wreath
For the commander that the call declared.

'Twas half-past ten when they drew up, prepared
To pass the river when the tide was low,
Some half hour later; mercilessly slow
The minutes crawled, and as each one dragged by,
Watches by scores, pulled out impatiently,
Bore witness to the torture of suspense,
As did sweat drops incessant and immense
Upon the foreheads.: Some men laughed aloud
Like madmen : Others, many years too proud
To bend before their Maker, strove to pray
In infantile and incoherent way,
Not unlike one who makes his first essay
Upon the ice. The very elements
Seeming to probe and augur the events
That threatened, threatened too in sympathy.
Dense thunder clouds wreathed and rolled in the sky
Like cannon smoke, and now and then a flash
Of lightning came before the general crash,
Like the chance shot that, fired by some vedette,
Brings on the action; and large drops of wet
Fell as a spent shot on the rear guard falls,
Fired at an outpost. Even animals
Sniffed something in the air : the horses' ears
Pricked and their nostrils quivered, and the steers
Reiv'd by foraging-parties from the pass
Ceased their contented munching of the grass.
At last the bugle blew,
And loud the clamour grew,

As the head columns plunged into the stream,
And French and English saw their " barrels " gleam.
They'd still well nigh a furlong more to go
Before they reached the outworks of the foe,
Part over rocks on which men scarce could stand
For slimy seaweed ; part o'er open sand,
Without a rise or scrub or pile of stones
To shield the storming-party from the guns,
Trained upon them from ev'ry embrasure
By gunners skilful and themselves secure.

One of the Glad are we that at last
three   That standing still is past,
Soldiers. Counting the piles of shells
     And guns and fire barrels.
     " Waiting's like lead " say I ;
     I think I'd rather die
     Than stand an hour more
     In rank upon that shore,
     Feeling my courage ebb
     As I made out the web
     They weave for us up there,
     Like spiders in their lair ;
     Though the stream is too deep
     And it's so hard to keep
     One's footing to the bank.
     Three file slipped and sank
     Upon our right just now ;

But the tide's getting low.
How these jagged rocks do cut
Whene'er one slips one's foot,
If one has a bad shoe;
My right sole came in two
As we marched down the glen
Back from Soraoreń.
Ah! now it's sand we're on,
I'm glad those rocks are done,
They were so slippery
With green seaweed, that we
Could scarcely stand upright,
Let alone march or fight.
I wonder why the deuce
They do not fire on us;
We must be quite half way
And all this time have they
Not fired a single shot.
It cannot be—they've not
Retreated silently?

By God, they have not.   See!
Full half our men are lower
Beneath that with'ring shower
Of canister and grape.
Will none of us escape?
Oh comrades, this is hell!
Did you see that bombshell

Blow half a company
Into eternity?
This hail of musketry
Will kill each mother's son.
Unless we can press on
And make our escalades.
Why they've fixed up swordblades
Just where we should alight,
Jumping down from this height;
And we cannot stop here,
Picked off by grenadier
And marksman as we stand.
It's no good to command
Fresh men to our support,
While this infernal fort
Remains impregnable;
They're just so much fuel
For gunpowder and shot.
The engineers should not
Have pronounced the breach good;
They never understood
How strong these ramparts be.
I do not think that we
Can leave this place alive,
However much we strive,
That curtain is so high;
But if we have to die,
We'll let the foe know why,

Although we have to go
Over the blades below
Up the face of that wall.
We know we can but fall,
Whether we stand or strike,
And I, for one, should like
To have the company
Of a foe when I die.
Come, messmates, don't despair,
We have yet time to dare ;
We are the forlorn-hope
And never should give up,
While life and legs are left ;
That was a big hole reft
In our ranks by that shell ;
'Twas close to me it fell,
And killed my right hand man,
Poor Ben Ridge ; he began
Life with a better start :
'Twill break old Ridge's heart,
Farmer Ridge of the mill.
He's looking for him still
At Yalding bridge, I'll bet,
Hoping to see him yet
Come back safe home again.
He 's sisters, too, poor Ben,
Crying because he's roaming,
And watching for his coming.

Well, he has ceased to roam
And gone to his long home.
It will be my turn next,
And nobody'll be vexed.
No one at Paddockwood
Thought I should come to good.
I don't mind the shot now,
I shall soon be laid low,
And the sooner to rest.
I never made a quest
Of what will follow after
Pain, lying still, or laughter.
Hullo ! there goes poor Shann,
He was my left-hand man,
And yet they don't take me,
The worst man of the three.
Well, he died best of all.
He was right on the wall
When he was bayoneted ;
I'll swear he wasn't dead
When the brute tossed him down
Upon the sword blades prone ;
And he'd a fair young wife,
The star of my dark life,
Pretty Marion Gill,
The pride of Hunton Hill—
Aye, and two little ones,
To mourn his far-off bones,

Bleached by Biscayan suns.
Well ! this Hell cannot last
Long : it must soon be past,
And we shall not know how.

What did that bugle blow ?
" Cease Firing." " Halt." " Lie down."
The end will now be known.
No, mates, be daunted not,
All is not over yet ;
Did you see that roundshot
Shiver the parapet ?
That was a Sixty-eight,
I know it by the jar ;
And those men will fire straight—
They fought at Trafalgar,
And shot down hundreds four,
And silenced ev'ry gun
On the great Bucentaure,
As they passed broadside on.

The men were falling at the greater breach
As fast as waves in winter on the beach ;
And at the lesser breach the Portuguese
Fell thickly, as the suffocated bees
Before the deadly and sulphureous blast ;
And succours added corpses, till at last
Remained nought but to signal—" Halt," " Lie down,"

And, when the forlorn hope was lying prone,
Over their heads to open fire once more,
At once from Chofre's bristling lines the roar
Of half a hundred great siege pieces burst,
And beat the ramparts down till no foe durst
Stay on the traverses that did command
Th' assaulted parapet on either hand.
And after no long time a mortar-shell,
Fired with uplifted muzzle, downward fell
Into the magazine of hand-grenades,
Fire-barrels, and bombshells, and such like aids
Wherewith the garrison had thought to hold
Their last retrenchments if the battle rolled
Over the breaches to the citadel.
And all of these, the moment the bomb fell,
Leapt up into the air in one bright flash,
And with it smoke, and after it a crash—
Just such a crash as when the Orient
High into air that August night was sent
When Nelson rode triumphant at the Nile;
And now, as then, for full a minute's while
With friend or enemy no cannon raged,
But when the smoke and dust were part assuaged,
With the appalling and unearthly cry
The British ever raise when battle's high,
The stormers leapt upon the first traverse.
Yet even then the gallant tirailleurs
Rallied, and on the top of the glacis

The tide of conflict flowed as doubtfully
As at the time when ebb and flood converge
And neither gives nor gains, and the waves surge.
Yet not for long—out-numbered and assailed
With that mad stubbornness that has prevailed
Against incredible odds in every clime,
The French shrunk backward, and in no long time
Over the lesser breach upon their flanks
Fell the fierce Portuguese, and broke their ranks.

The Soldier.   I thought that Sixty-eight
              Would let them feel its weight;
              See how the parapet
              Is battered down by it.
              It can't be many hours
              Before the place is ours,
              From keep to waterline.

              My God! they've sprung a mine
              I'm not afraid to die
              But now—I don't know why—
              It seems so hard to go
              The moment that the foe
              Is likely to give in.
              I don't know what is sin,
              And don't know how to pray,
              And, if I knew the way,
              Don't know what good 'twould be.

It seems an age to me
Before we are blown up.
O God that there were hope !

No ! I've escaped this brew,
What was't the bugle blew?
"Advance." "Double." "Charge !" now
We'll pay them blow for blow.
That was a rare old thrust
That made him bite the dust.
I heard the bayonet squish
As it ripped through the flesh,
And felt my barrel prest
Right up against his chest :
That pays for poor young Ridge
Who lived by Yalding bridge.
This thirsty bayonet
Has Shann to pay for yet,
And pretty Marion—
Aye, and each little one.
How thick the Frenchmen fall !
Our blood's up, one and all,
With standing neath that wall
And being killed like sheep,
While they stood on the steep,
As safe as men in mail,
Just waiting to impale
Us as we strove to scale.

'Twas my turn to assault
When the call sounded " Halt,"
Or I should not be here.
    Why here's the grenadier
That threw Shann's body down ;
I know him by the frown
Made by a sabre scar
Received in some old war.
Perhaps he's not quite dead,
He'd best be bayoneted ;
Take that, and that ! I'll swear
His eyes woke to a stare
When first I ran him through :
That's more than he will do
When he's run through again.
What is that?   Have the foe
Surrendered to our men ?
Then, comrades, to sack ho !

O, surely ne'er shall phantasy recite,
A tragedy to emulate that night ;
Mid houses sacked and flaming to the sky,
Arose unintermittently the cry
Of wives and tender maidens suffering
The wrong of wrongs that poets blush to sing.
Age shielded not, nor rank, nor unripe youth
From lust of the outragers ; nor did ruth
Hinder from treading on a father's corse,

Or bayoneting a husband's breast, to force
The womanhood he strove from lust to shield.
And to and fro the brutal soldiers reeled
From drink to rape, and rape to drink again,
Like fiends let loose from Hell, rather than men,
As, mad with liquor and befouled with blood,
They hurled with frantic glee into the mud
Pictures and plate, and antique jewellery,
And rich apparel, and rare tapestry,
As they had been so many packs of wool,
And drank raw spirits by the bonnet-full
As they got up the kegs, and stove them in
With hideous triumph and more hideous din,
And mingled the fierce fluid with the gore
Of all who said them nay, or stood before
The drunkard or seducer at his work.
While with wan glare the frequent lightning-fork
Put the tall flames in shade and made the scene
Look trebly devilish, and, in between,
The thunder crashes drowned the voice of crime.
In gentler times, it well might look sublime
To see the flashes point the Pyrenees
And multiply reflections on the seas ;
But now it seemed as if the Powers of air
Thundered in sympathy, and came to share
In the new Hell.   In vain the officers,
In spite of mutinous and gnashing curse,
Strove to rein in the men, and form again

Into some order, and as much in vain
Spoke of the Castle, yet intact, where lay
With fresh battalions the undaunted Rey,
Waiting, perchance, to fall upon the foe,
And retribution wring for that day's woe.
The men, unmoved, murdered and pillaged on
And outraged, amid moan, and moan, and moan.

The Soldier. You, sir, pray where were you,
        You with your epaulettes,
        When from the parapets
        The grape rained down and slew
        Us poor chaps by the score?
        I daresay with the staff
        Upon the further shore,
        Having a sneering laugh
        At some unfeeling jest,
        While we poor devils, prest
        Upon the open sand,
        Went down hand over hand.
          You call us savages—
        So'd you be an' you please,
        If you'd been penned all day
        And shot and shot away
        Without striking a blow,
        And seen a bloody foe
        Toss on the pikes below
        The bodies of your friends

Before they met their ends.
Don't talk to me of wives !
Did they think of Shann's wife
When they tossed down poor Shann
On the pikes, a live man ?
Don't talk to me of lives,
Tell me ! wasn't Shann's life
Worth any enemy's ?
Will she have dryer eyes
Than a Frenchwoman would ?
What'ud her womanhood
Have been worth if they'd won,
And then had fallen on
Her in a conquered town ?
Because her eyes are brown
Would they have let her go ?
Would a bosom of snow
Have hindered them, forsooth,
From soiling her fair youth ?
Man, man, we are but men,
Though we wear a red coat
And march into a moat
Twenty feet deep and drown,
If we are ordered down
In battle's hour.   But when
The battle's o'er and won,
A chap must have his run ;
And harkee, sir, I will.

Pull out your sword and kill
Me, an' you like, who stood
Against the French all day ;
I can't fight, an' I would.
I threw my piece away,
And can no weapon get
Except a bayonet.
" Drink " did you say? Why not ?
I haven't had a pot
Of drink this long month's space.
" Drunk !" you know by my face !
Well, and if I were worse,
I shouldn't care a curse.
I've done my work to-day,
And mean to have my play.
" Murder !" Didn't they kill
Poor Ridge, of Yalding Mill
With a bursting bombshell,
While we were in that hell
Under their parapet,
Before the Sixty-eight
Smashed up the traverses ?
Are their lives more than his ?
I ran through my first man
For throwing down poor Shann ;
The next for young Ben Ridge,
And the next for old Ben
That lives by Yalding bridge,

One for each sister, and then
Two for Shann's bonny wife,
And took a Frenchman's life
For either little one.
I didn't stop to count
How many more went down
When first we stormed the town.
Lord! how the blood does mount
When one gets a fair rush
And a bayonet push
After standing for hours
Riddled with steady showers
Of grape and canister.
No offence to you, sir,
But men will be men here:
And not to interfere
Is all that you can do,
And no disgrace to you,
Nothing will cure to-night
But the chill of daylight.

Will asked the two betrothed to stay
After the rest had gone away,
Wishing to make apologies
About the bittern's obsequies,
And after these were laughed off, all
Lingered awhile about the hall.
It seemed so odd to Will to think

That Lil, who yet was on the brink
Of girlhood and of womanhood,
Was soon to leave their home for good.
To him she still was just a child
As bright, ingenuous and wild,
And he was curious to see
Her with her lover quietly
To form his own conjectures of
Their future happiness and love.

Reader, observe the tender touch
Of nature which delights so much.
To Lil it was a luxury
To sit upon her lover's knee
Before her brother openly.
It showed her that the love she prized
Was regular and recognised.
She knew that if it did look bold
No human being would be told,
As far as Will's tongue was concerned,
And her soft heart within her burned
To symbolise in outward ways
The love which so fulfilled her days.

December 31st.

To-day they voted a battue
And hunt among the kangaroo.
Himself a horseman bold and good
As very few who ever rode,
Will on the hunt cold water threw.
"At all events it would not do
For the Professor, or indeed
For Chesterfield, to ride full speed
Through the thick scrub with fallen trees
And rabbit-burrows thick as bees.
And he would be much loath to lend
His worst horse to his dearest friend
For such a freak. Of course if Lil
And Kit and Margaret and Phil
Liked to ride their own nags they could,
Or lend them just as they thought good.
But in his judgment it was best—
At any rate he would suggest—
To get a shooting-party up,
And send some men ahead to stop
And some men back to drive the game
Right past. He knew the tracks they came
To drink and feed, and easily
Could post guns just where they passed by."
"Why not do both?" asked Kit, who was
Ready upon the slightest cause

To ride wherever there was risk
Of breaking neck or limb, as brisk
In courting danger as her wit
Was ready in eluding it.
"Why not do both? We might divide
Some post ourselves, and others ride
To help the men. I volunteer."
"And I," cried Phil just after her,
Fired with the possibilities
Which might from the rencontre rise
(And which shrewd Kit had duly weighed
But thought she could contrive t' evade
On plea of 'beating' properly
Whenever he came too close by).
Phil lent the horse which Hall rode on,
First offered to Maud Morrison,
Who rode sometimes but "did not care,"
So she said, meaning "did not dare"
To ride that day. The only one
Who did not go but would have gone
Was Lil, who as above was told
When upon horseback was as bold
As she was timid otherwise.
But she was met with pleading eyes
By the Professor, when she glanced
In question, and discountenanced.
The bare idea of the ride
His active fancy terrified
With nightmare dreams of accidents,
Nor did he like experiments.

    *   *   *   *

Will, a good bushman, knew each track
The kangaroo would likely take
When beaten up, and spread his force
At vantage-points along the course.
He took the first point, that his gun
Might warn the others.   Further on
Was Chesterfield, and Lachlan Smith
Still further.   Lil was posted with
Her lover—one good reason was
That they enjoyed it, one because
Lil bred to country life had eyes
More open to its mysteries
Than the Professor, and the two
Were posted last, because Will knew
That folks so prepossessed as they
Might hear a gun go off all day
And hardly notice.   While they lay
Crouched in the fern, they watched the life
With which the forest depths are rife,—
The cold snake coiling in the sun
On any open space ; the dun
And drowsy ' native bear ' at ease,
Wedged in high forks of lofty trees ;
The blue and scarlet lory sitting
Close by his much-loved mate, or flitting
With a discordant scream between
The ' lightwood's ' dense and sombre green,
Rivalled in his metallic blue
By ' warbler ' cock ' superb ' in hue,
But little as a common wren
With a most unpretentious hen ;

The jackass, perched upon a branch
Of a bare gum-tree, who would launch
From time to time unearthly peals
Of laughter, watching as it steals
And darts alternately, his prey,
The common lizard, while there lay
Seemingly sleeping in the heat,
A huge iguana 'neath his feet.
The insect-world was everywhere,—
Flies and mosquitoes in the air,
Tyrannical and trumpeting;
Spiders of all kinds ravelling
In filmy threads each bush and tree;
Ants all round far as one could see
Pursuing their eternal march,
Coming and going through an arch
Made by two pebbles in the ground,
Or crossing a ravine profound,
Nothing so little or so great
To baffle them—as stern as Fate.
But strange ! in all the hum of life
With which the forest-morn was rife,
No single note of song was heard
Like that the yellow-billed, black bird
Raises when cherries turn to red
In Kent: nor aught was heard instead
Save the deep-throated native thrush
Calling out from the leafy bush
Of some tree-top his ' who are you,'
Clear-toned but tuneless, and the new
Incomparable chant, bell-like

Resounded by the magpie-shrike.
　At last they came, the kangaroo,
Not in a drove but one or two,
And these not the great 'foresters'
But small 'brush-kangaroo,' with furs
Of reddish tinge, not that there was
A dearth of them there but because
The riders, five of them in all,
Two men and Phil and Kit and Hall
Had failed to keep the proper line
Which constituted Will's design.
Phil was in fault : he was to ride
Upon the left on the outside
The shooters being on the right
And the 'stops' posted opposite.
And this was how it came about :
Kit was next Phil and he fell out,
Attracted by her pretty face,
To be near her ; and thus a space
Was left uncovered on the left
By which the game with instinct deft
Broke sideways out of the cordon.
Only a few were hurried on,
In their blind flight unnoticing
The gap left open on the wing,
And Will had settled two of them,
And Chesterfield one after him,
Bringing them down to one or two,
Which scarcely as much leapt as flew,
So scared were they when they came up
To where the last gun had to stop.

He fired two cartridges away
After the heltering-skeltering prey
Without result, and then crouched still
Until he heard a shout from Will
Calling to lunch, which he discussed
With pleasure, tempered by disgust
Attendant on his ill-success,—
Doomed to be transient none the less.
   Lunch over, when the rest had gone
Partly to leave the two alone,
Partly to try the ground once more
In the same order as before
Beginning from the other side,
With Phil and Kit told off to ride
On the two flanks to quite prevent
Any such tender incident
As that which spoiled the morning's sport.
   The morning had left Philip Forte
More hopelessly in love than e'er
With Kit. She looked so queenly fair
In her close-fitting habit made
Of light-grey tweed; and in the glade
With her blood dancing as she rode
Full speed, no mortal woman could
Maintain an iciness of mien;
The magic of the time and scene
And motion lured her back into
A mood that really was her true
And natural mood, and she received
Advances with what he believed
Was wakening love, but which in truth

Was just the heartiness of youth
Laid open with excitement's wand.
　In course of time the lovers fond
The old adage did illustrate,
That he who can afford to wait
Must win.　For, as they sat at ease
Under the overhanging trees
On cushions from the waggonette,
Still lingering where lunch was set,
One of the horses tethered near
Began to snort and prick his ear.
Lil, a good bushman, noticed it,
And bade him load his gun and sit
As still as death, and soon the sound
Of a dull thud upon the ground
Confirmed suspicions, and there hopped
Almost to where they were, and stopped,
Looking about suspiciously
At the strange sights which met its eye,
A full-grown 'old man' kangaroo.
"Shoot it," said Lil, and full and true
Into its head her lover poured
A charge of buckshot, on the sward
Dropping his prey, without a kick
As stiff and lifeless as a stick.
Lil first felt glad that it was shot,
And then she wished that it were not.
Glad that her lover had obtained
What he so much desired, and pained
For the poor beast, whose great dark eyes
Pled mutely for her sympathies.

At last she gave adherence to
Her lover, not the kangaroo.

      *   *   *   *

Ida was queen that night, and made
Her choice of subject ' Love,' and bade
The lover concentrate his tale
Not on the female but the male.
" You've given us a picture of
A pretty English girl in love
In Ethel.   Show us if you can
The feelings of an Englishman
In the same sweet predicament. "
" Bravo ! " exclaimed with one consent
Kit and the statesman, and the first
Whispered, " I did not think she durst,
Has not she splendid impudence
To sally thus at his expense ? "
    Cobham took refuge in a smile,
And, thinking for a little while,
Gave them a tale half revery
And half of it reality.

SAPPHO.

(A REVERY.)

The full moon glitters on the sand,
The North Sea ripples on the strand,
The low cliff's shadow from above
Falls on a little landlock'd cove,
Which, deep and dang'rous to the edge,

Mines underneath the chalky ledge,
Save where the bank, with gentle sink,
Slopes downward to the water's brink.
Here Harold stood : the night was clear,
And through the purple atmosphere
The stars shone brightly, and the sea
Sang chorus to his rhapsody :
A man whom all might happy deem,
And women love, and men esteem ;
Full broad of shoulder, strong of arm,
And deaf to anger or alarm,
But chivalrous in hastiness
To champion trouble or distress ;
As great in spirit as in frame,
In danger and distress the same,
With wild, dark, handsome, haunting face—
And strength in manhood serves for grace :
Able was he to hold his own,
And worthy admiration ;
Accustom'd since he scarce could stand
To the stern pastimes of his land :
At first to shoulder off the stool
The other little boys at school,
And then to wrestle and to fight
With ten-year rivals, his delight ;
Then competition took the place
Of stand-up fighting face to face ;
There were brave battles to be fought

In beating other boys at sport;
And as the rolling years went on
Great glory in such sports he won;
Fours to true leg, straight spanking drives
Snick'd twos and threes, clean cuts for fives,
Fast ripping balls, well on the wicket,
Made him renown'd in Rugby cricket.
Hot 'hacks' exchanged, 'tries' dearly bought;
A hero in the sterner sport.
He'd stalk'd the red deer over Highland rocks;
He'd 'taken' untried fences for the fox;
In Kentish copses, 'neath an autumn sun,
The largest bag had fallen to his gun;
In Norway rivers, waist-deep in the flood,
Salmon of weight had yielded to his rod:
Alone, afoot, on many a weary day,
O'er steep wet moor and featureless highway,
He strode to fields of unforgotten fights
Of Rupert's cavaliers and Clifford's knights;
To storied castles shatter'd in the war
'Twixt Crown and Commons, minsters where of yore
Dunstan and Baeda fed the sacred light
Of learning in the long dark English night;
To abbeys rich with knightly founders' bones,
And gifts of bygone heroes and kings' sons;
To great cathedrals hallow'd by the pray'r
Of great dead men; to cities famed and fair;
To torrents foaming, fretting, falling fast,

And mighty rivers slowly sailing past
By stately halls and immemorial trees ;
To lonely wolds and humming village leas,
Green downs, and grey gaunt mountains, and broad
　　plains
Strewn with old chieftains' tombs and fallen fanes ;
To silent reed-fring'd lake and lone sea-shore,
As silent, save for surf and storm wind's roar.
He knew the names of all known stars in heaven—
The heralds of the morning and the even ;
He knew the names of all the birds that fly,
And beasts that range beneath the Northern sky,
And many fish that in the north seas ply ;
He knew the gauzy denizens of air,
And had a hoard wherein the rich and rare
Of daily butterfly and nightly moth
Were ranged together, and he knew in troth
The name of every flow'r that wood and field
From Cornwall to Northumberland do yield.

Ballads he knew, and many a legend old
In knightly Kent and daring Devon told,
And many a border-boast and roundelay
Sung in the good green wood : these he would say
Word by word, line by line, and verse by verse,
After the croonings of a fond old nurse,
Who had nought else to teach him : these he knew,
And sought out many other when he grew,

In dingy quarto bought at fusty stall
Or 'neath old cottage prints fantastical.
   Oft far into the night he converse held
With the great minds and noble hearts of eld—
Caedmon and Mallory, and old Geoffry,
The sire and sieur of English poesy ;
Spenser and More and Shakspere, England's voice,
In whom the ears of ages shall rejoice ;
Sweet Sidney, Beaumont, Fletcher, 'rare old Ben,'
And glorious Milton, brave John Bunyan,
Pepys, Evelyn, Clarendon, Addison,
Dick Steele, Defoe and Swift—these he would con,
And Keats and fairy Shelley, who could tell
The sadness of all happiness too well ;
And Landor, he to whom 'twas given to show
The longings and the life of long ago.
   And often to these meetings at midnight
Came old school friends he'd studied with delight,
Not diligence : Homer the editor,
And Hesiod the old, and many more ;
Dear babbling, loosely-learn'd Herodotus,
Euripides, Sophocles, Æschylus,
Plato and Aristotle ; and the soft
Anacreon came with them ; nor less oft
Came sage Lucretius and Cicero,
Virgil and witty Horace, Gallio
And legendary Livy ; oft too came
The second sire of poetry—a flame

From his own Hell was burning in that breast,
Whence the triunal vision was express'd—
Condemn'd, his love unknown and dead, to roam
In poor and painful exile from his home.
And with him came Messer Boccaccio,
Full of the loves and jests of long ago;
And many a bard who'd listed to his tales,
And sung them o'er again, and one from Wales,
And one from Alcalà, and many more
Whose names were writ in fire, in days of yore.

And sometimes, when he heard the stirring hum
Of music or great shoutings, there would come
Heroes and hosts: Herman and Hannibal,
Etzel, the Cid, Roland of Roncesvalles,
Harold of Hastings, Richard Lion-heart
And Edward the Black Prince; nor far apart,
Hawkins and Drake, Raleigh and Frobisher,
And the great Howard, Ironside Oliver
And his Ironsides, and Rupert, hand-on-sword,
And Buonaparte, and he who cross'd the ford
Against advice and conquer'd on that day
When he won Plassey and England India;
And those Six Hundred heroes.   And at times,
Releas'd by midnight's necromantic chimes,
Came the true lovers and wild souls of yore—
Dauntless Medea, one from Naxos' shore,
Helen and light-heart Paris, Psyche true,

Aspasia and the masterman who drew
More glory from her sweetness than the sway
Of Athens in her hour, and Thaïs gay,
Who ruled the world's commander : with these came
Dido and lone Iarbas, hearts of fame,
That lov'd at odds ; and some of later name—
Abelard, Heloïse, and Rosamond,
And Castile's Eleanor, whose love was found
Proof against poison, and the Florentine
Who bore deep graven on his heart divine
The little maid twice seen through years of power
And years of pain : and many a rare hour
Came the white Queen of Scots.　Here all who fell
Victims to service true, or lov'd too well,
Were welcome, for his wild heart long'd to know
Such love as beauty tender'd long ago.

　　Indeed, he ev'ry gift could boast
But the three gifts he valued most—
Wealth to pet beauty, beauty's self,
Won for his own sake, not for pelf,
And laurels of a poet : he
Enough had tasted of all three
To thirst for more.　To many a maid
His fancy 'd for a moment stray'd ;
Blue eyes and hazel, grey and brown,
Had answer'd frankly to his own ;
Auburn and flaxen, black and gold,

Had mesh'd his heart in glossy fold ;
But ever came an undertone
Of something wanting in each one.
The lady of his choice should be
Sublime in her simplicity,
Of lowly mind and high estate,
And fairy-light in grace and gait ;
One who would try to understand
Whate'er he wrote, whate'er he plann'd ;
With fitful anger for defence
Against abus'd obedience,
And just sufficient patience
To obviate unjust offence ;
With beauty intellectual,
The rarest witchery of all,
And curly clustering wealth of hair
Indented by a forehead fair,
And broad and creamy ; thoughtful eyes,
Open in innocent surprise,
Melting in pity, fired in wrath,
Pouring the soul's whole secret forth
In love, not unacquaint with tears.
She must have tender girlish fears,
And a soft voice, with elfin mirth,
And presence equal to her birth ;
She must be coy—the more they cost
More dear they are, the dearest most ;
But when she yields let her confess

With all the gentler tenderness,
And hungry kiss and hot caress.
Passion and love walk hand in hand :
Content is imitation bland
For widowers and second wives,
And men whose ledgers are their lives ;
Youth's passion-flow'r is delicate
And, blighted, blossoms not till late.

Sooth'd by the sweet salt soughing breeze,
He linger'd over shapes like these,
Now peering from the ledge above
Into the clear depth of the cove,
Now gazing upward at a star,
And now across the sea afar,
To a lithe schooner-yacht that lay,
Nodding her slim masts, on the bay ;
When suddenly he heard the plash,
And saw the phosphorescent flash
Of dipping oars, and then a skiff,
Making the shore beneath the cliff.
A muffled lady and old man
Sat in the stern-sheets ; soon it ran
To where the coast with gradual sink
Sloped downwards to the water's brink.
The old man rose, and lightly sprung
Ashore, and safe.   The shallop swung
Just as his daughter leapt, and she

N

Sank in the clear depth of the sea ;
She swerv'd and sank without a sound,
And as she fell the scarf unwound
That veil'd her features, and laid bare
A sweet fair face and gold of hair
Crowning it ; as she sank she smiled,
And shot a glance intense and wild
Up at the ledge where Harold stood.
He in a strange ecstatic mood
Was gazing downwards at the flood,
And the wet face, which seem'd to be
That of a goddess of the sea.
Then in he plung'd, she gripp'd his arms
And, in the terror that disarms
The mind of reason, dragg'd him down,
As Sirens in the legend drown
   The victims of their song.
He thought in that short minute's space
Of his long start and ill-run race,
   Of all the waste and wrong
That crowded in his misspent life,
Of all the soarings and the strife
   Of his foreshorten'd day,
Of ev'ry uncompleted aim,
Of unachiev'd desire of fame,
   And chances slipp'd away :
And ere his senses lost control·
He thought of his immortal soul,

And felt he could not pray.

   *   *   *   *   *

THE DREAM.

He, standing by the landlock'd cove,
Built airy palaces of love,
And, leaning over, strove to peer
Beneath the starlit waters clear,
When suddenly arose a maid
Out of the depth, and, unafraid,
Swam near him, and in sweet, soft voice
Bade Harold welcome, and rejoice.
" At last," she said, " my love, thou'rt come :
Thou hast been long away from home."
He look'd at her, but could not tell
What maid it was that lov'd him well,
And said, " Who are you, sweet ?" but she—
" Wilt thou renew thy cruelty,
Erst cruel Phaon ? know'st thou not
Thy bride, thy Sappho ?   From my grot
Beneath the ocean oft have I
Gazed upward at the shore and sky
To see thee once again ; and now
Thou'rt come.   I pray thee, dear heart, vow
That thou wilt ne'er forsake me more
For idle dalliance on the shore,
But seek in love's unfailing arms
A shelter from the world's alarms,

And pillow'd on a white warm breast
Lull thine o'er-labour'd head to rest."
   He edg'd a step toward the cove,
Irresolute 'twixt life and love ;
She swam a stroke toward the shore,
Pleading and beckoning the more,
And said, " I loved those wilful curls
As none among the Lesbian girls :
No maid in Mitylene 'd prize
Gems, as I prized those glad brown eyes—
I, who the love of man defied,
Offered my beauty to your pride,
And you despised it ; then I wail'd
And all my joy in living fail'd,
And oft I sought a lonely rock
That quiver'd with the billows' shock,
And bore my burthen to the breeze,
And sang my sorrows to the seas ;
And last I plung'd, in hope to be
Reprieved by death from misery.

" But the mermen pined for the love of me,
  As I sang to the sea and sky ;
And those who are loved by kings of the sea
  May be drown'd, but cannot die.

" Their kisses I loath'd, and I loath'd their love,
  The more as they prov'd more true ;

And all the day long I would rove and rove,
   Watching and waiting for you.

" Then lay down your weary head in my arms,
   And you shall a merman be,
And reign as a king in the careless calms
   Of the fathomless sapphire sea."

Harold.

" But I have joys I cannot leave :
The glow of morning and of eve,
   The glory of the noon ;
The golden sun that shines on high,
The stars embroider'd on the sky,
   The silver of the moon."

Sappho.

" But the sun shines through the breast of the blue,
   And moon-finger'd waves are fair,
And the stars we view reflected anew
   On the gold of mermaid hair."

Harold.

" But I have other joys than these :
The cliffs and mountains, and the breeze
   That freshens round their tops ;
The valleys with their kirtles green,
The uplands with their shoulders sheen
   And coronal of copse."

Sappho.

" There are hills and valleys below the deep
    Far fairer than any of earth ;
And the winds of your mountains wake and sleep,
    In the ocean that gives them birth."

Harold.

" But I have fairy flow'rs that rise
Fresh from their winter obsequies
    To decorate the spring ;
And others of a later day
To grace the summer, and delay
    The autumn's taking wing."

Sappho.

" The sea-flowers are more glorious far,
    And they never sleep or die ;
Our anemones wear the shape of a star,
    And hue of a sunset sky."

Harold.

" And I have groves whose living shade
Is canopy and colonnade
    Beneath an August sun ;
Choice garden trees with fruitage fine,

And evergreens that never pine
  When August days are done."

Sappho.

" And under the sea there are gardens sweet,
  And coral groves red and white ;
We know not the changes of cold and heat,
  But love the sun for his light."

Harold.

" The birds I love so fleet and fair
That glitter through the sunny air,
  And warble in the dawn ;
The insect-radiance of May,
Whose dotage closes with the day
  That saw their brightness born."

Sappho.

" We have beautiful shapes and tuneful shells
  In our wondrous world below ;
But the glories of ocean no one tells,
  And none but the mermen know."

Harold.

" But most of all I love to stand
On each grey castle of our land,

And nodding Norman keep,
Telling with scatter'd walls and scars
A rugged tale of great old wars
And warriors long asleep :
To muse on moss-hid arch and aisle
Of desecrate Cistercian pile
And fane of long ago ;
To wander through a village street
Trod by a great man's childish feet
While yet his lot was low ;
To gaze across a moor whereon
A famous victory was won
Or some stout hero fell ;
And often have I fondly roved
Where two wild lovers met and lov'd,
Not wisely, but too well."

Sappho.

" We have no castles in ruin revered,
No abbeys of long ago,
No villages where great men were rear'd
While yet their lot was low.
But we have some rare old battle-grounds
Where heroes were kill'd at bay,
And buried chiefs without burial mounds,
And trystings of lovers gay.
Then lay down your wearied head in my arms,
And you shall a merman be,

And reign as a king in the careless calms
  Of the fathomless sapphire sea."

Harold.

"But under the sea, love, under the sea,
  What do you do for the clear blue sky?"

Sappho.

"O! the clear blue sea is a sky to me,
  And our heaven is not too high."

Then in he plung'd: she drew him down,
As sirens in the legend drown
    The victims of their melody.
The waters gurgled in his ears,
    He deem'd that he must die;
But Sappho sooth'd away his fears
    With kisses wooingly.
Down, down they sank until they reach'd
A sapphire-vaulted cavern beach'd
With jet and shells of pearl; the walls
Were cataracts and waterfalls.
Here they abode full lovingly,
And smoothly the quick days sped by.
Sometimes he sits upon the rocks,
Upgathering her elfin locks;
Sometimes she sits upon his knee,
And sings him anthems of the sea;

Sometimes upon the sand he lies,
Gazing at sea-blue steadfast eyes
   That concentrate on him ;
And sometimes for an hour's space
He dallies with a fair, fond face
   And body rounded slim.
She tells him legends of the deep,
And shows him where the mermen keep
   Their fleet of founder'd ships,
And where their milliard army lies
Of skeletons with hollow eyes
   And grinning jaws for lips.
But most of all she's used to tell
Of those old hours she lov'd so well,
   The hours of Lesbian song ;
To call back some sad roundelay,
That wiled away an elderday
   Whereon he linger'd long ;
To call back how it sooth'd to rove,
And tell the breezes of her love
   And waters of her woes ;
To whisper consummated bliss,
And seal her whisper with a kiss,
   And sink in sweet repose.

Thus sped they many a joyous day
In amorous and peaceful play,
Glad of a respite from the fears

Of eager and ambitious years.
But last it fell that Sappho's cheek
Grew hollow and her body weak :
He saw and griev'd until she broke
The silence, and the dull truth spoke :
   " We have no souls, dear love,
For had we souls we could not live
Without the elements that give
   The life they live above—
The daily drink, the daily fare,
The sweet and all-sustaining air."

" What matter," he cried, " though we have no soul
   We shall live as long as the earth,
Without the millstone of care and control
   Which hangs round the neck from birth.

" We have all the wonders of deep and bay,
   And the heaven is ours above,
As much as the mortals who toil all day
   And have only the night for love.

" And if no future in heaven be ours
   When the earth is ended, we've this—
We can make a heaven of earthly hours,
   And sweeten our end with a kiss."

Sappho.

   " Though love is good and gracious ease,

Life is for nobler ends than these :
To build impregnably a name
And force unwilling grants from fame ;
To gain great victories, and give
A wise example how to live ;
To give your country liberty,
Or teach her patriots how to die ;
To chronicle your finest thought
For generations to be taught ;
With practice and with preaching win
A sinful people from their sin,
To point your tale and wing your song
As arrows against wrath and wrong."

Though he for love and ease was fain,
His nobler nature woke again :
"Teach me, my love," he said, " once more
To win the souls we had before,
What toils attain, what pains restore."

" It is writ in the Book of the Sea," she saith,
    " That a merman a soul may gain
Who snatches the life of a man from death
    Or a maiden's love can attain."
Then to the landlock'd cove they swam,
And when they to the inlet came
He saw a drowning maiden sink
In the clear depth beside the brink.
He seem'd to clasp her, as before,

And bear her breathing to the shore,
And, lo ! the maid in his embrace
Wore Sappho's form and Sappho's face.

The End of the Dream.

He woke : beside his pillow stood
More perfect in her womanhood
   The lady of his vision,
Her lips half parted for a smile
   In sweetest indecision,
Whether to fly or bide the while
   He ask'd of his position.
She stay'd : it needs no Chaldee seer
Or Arabic astrologer
   To guess their conversation ;
The meaning of the mystery
   Needs no interpretation ;
We leave the after-history
   To your imagination.

The first time that they were alone
After this tale of his was done,
Lil questioned him if he were not
Himself the hero of the plot.
To which he answered, " No indeed
I am no hero, but I read
The kind of books I make him choose,

And like the same things as he does."

*   *   *   *

That evening they had a dance,
Due chiefly to the circumstance
That Phil was so in love that he
Had come and listened patiently
Right through the tale to be with Kit,
And had, when Cobham finished it,
Suggested dancing in the hope
That she might be induced to stop
As a spectator, purposing
When he had "done the proper thing"
By waltzing a few rounds, to watch
His opportunity to catch
Her at some moment, when so placed
That she could hardly with good taste
Leave him, and then to make best use
Of what the parley might produce.
Kit saw the danger, yet scarce knew
What there remained for her to do,
The clicking of a billiard-ball
Told her that Lachlan Smith and Hall
Were playing billiards, so that she
Could not go thither decently.
She felt that Phil would follow her
And hang about her everywhere,
So, when she saw him pause, she went
Dnd much to Will's astonishment
Asked him if he would care to dance,
Believing this her only chance.
  She knew that if she danced with Will

She might be forced to dance with Phil,
But then one need not hear a word
Excepting of one's own accord
When one is dancing, and she meant,
When it was over, to prevent
A confidential tête-à-tête
By asking him to take her straight
To the piano to express
Her overpowering thankfulness
To the musician—there to stay,
Chatting the interval away
Until another dance began,
As fixed as is Aldeboran.
The plan succeeded and did not,
Like many things which wise folks plot.
Phil could not have his tête-à-tête
And Kit but hurried on her fate.

Of course as soon as she and Will
Their dance had finished, up came Phil
With Maud upon his arm to ask
That he might have the next—a task
Which Maud by no means liked, and Kit
As little liked the granting it.

Kit's dancing, as the reader knows,
Was perfect in its stately pose
And docile movement, light of tread
And true of step, with the fair head
Carried as though she were a queen
Although so gracious in its mien

Phil looked a thorough gentleman,
And danced so well as few men can,

And Kit artistic pleasure drew
From dancing with her foe, so true
And perfect was the unison
With which they moved, that everyone
(Excepting poor Maud Morrison,
Who could not to herself deny
Her own inferiority)
Paused to look on with praise unfeigned,
Lil above all, who thought her friend
The autotype of elegance,
And bade her lover ask a dance,
Saying that Kit danced best of all
The girls she'd seen at school or ball,
Which seemed to him a reason why
He should not with her wish comply.
" She will not care to dance with me,
I can't do the new step, and she
Does it so irreproachably."
" Kit can dance all," was Lil's reply,
" And so could Maud if she would try,
And Kit is far too highly bred
To speak as rudely as Maud did."
    So he asked Kit, who answered " yes "
With such a frank sweet graciousness,
Adapting her own step to his
So furtively and with such ease
That he was ready to endorse
Lil's eulogy with tenfold force.
    Kit was a girl who if she chose
Might have led most men ' by the nose,'
And she her safety found to-night

In coming down from her cold height,
And being womanly to all,
Which gave her a brief interval
From present dread, but hurried on
The climax.   Phil danced off and on
With her throughout the evening,
In every fibre quivering
With a new sense of fierce delight,
Interpreting the opposite
Of her intentions, and in fear
Lest he should not obtain her ear
While she was in this gentle mood.
Poor Kit ! Anticipations wooed
That which she strove to guard against.
Poor Phil ! who dreamed they evidenced
Surrender and not armament.
And yet both went to bed content,
She that she'd beaten off the foe,
He that he'd but to strike the blow
To find the fortress at his feet
On any terms which he thought meet.

January 1st.

In Melbourne the great " Champion "
Upon each New-Year's day is run,
And every little country town
Likes to have races of its own
Or sports or fairs upon that day.
　Some half-a-dozen miles away
Was a small place to which the Fortes
Went every year to see the sports.
The sports were nothing much to see,
But it bred cordiality
Between them and the people round
If they were seen upon the ground.
And Will was judge, because he'd been
"A C. U. A. C. Blue." *　The scene,
If not attractive to the eye,
Presented a variety :—
Merry-go-rounds, and galleries
For rifle shooting with a prize
Which no one ever won, potshots
A penny each at cocoa-nuts,
Aunt Sally, try-your-strength-machines,
And here and there, behind the scenes,
The 'three-card trick,' 'hat-trick,' 'roulette,'

---

* *I.e.*, one of the representatives of Cambridge University in
the Inter-University Athletic Sports at Lillie Bridge.

And other snares by sharpers set
The simple country folk to gull,
Though dupes were not too plentiful.
And then there were the usual shows—
Fat women, dwarfs, gigantic sows,
A six-legged calf, and mermaid stuffed,
The whole inordinately puffed.
The sports were mostly handicaps
Distinguished chiefly by the traps
Which runners from a distance set
Undue advantages to get.
In nearly every race some tried
To have some one disqualified
For false name, false performances,
Or other insincerities.

    The handicap draws larger fields,
But in most other ways it yields
To open contests for the best.
Handicaps are no real test.
All that they generally mean
Is that the handicapper 's been
Ill-posted on the winner's form.
You could distinguish by the storm
Of acclamations which outburst
When local runners came in first.

    For educated lookers-on
There would not have been any fun,
But for an aboriginal
Who started (without fees at all)
For every race—one of the wrecks
Whom white men's vices, without checks

Which white men have, were dragging down
Post-haste to his perdition,
A blear-eyed, whiskey-sodden wretch,
Often too tottering to fetch
A pail of water to a horse.
He almost reeled about the course—
A contrast to the crowd, who were
Far soberer and steadier
Than such a crowd oft is elsewhere.
The crowning merriment was when
This poor degraded specimen
Of the old rulers of the place
Had started in a hurdle race,
And, jumping too close, sat upon
The hurdle-rails as he came down.

* * * *

But only Will of all the Fortes
Paid much attention to the sports.
Phil was too busy with his suit,
Kit with contrivances astute
To fence it off.   Lil and her lover
Wished to go ere it was half over,
And the rest scarce attended more
Than did the interested four.
The two old folks had stayed at home,
Thinking it better not to come,
The neighbours being quite content
If any of their party went.
Ida had grappled Chesterfield,
Who seemed agreeable to yield.
Indeed the cheerful little dame,

Always so kind, always the same,
And always fashionably dressed
(In fashions that became her best),
Was calculated to engage
A politician of his age
And corrigible bachelor
No less, if not indeed much more,
Than a mere girl whose prettiness
Was her sole claim to his address.
And these two bandied chaff all day
In what Will called a reckless way,
When he came back to steal a munch
Of their drawn-out, luxurious lunch.

    The barrister was trying on
Blandishments with Maud Morrison,
But found her less amenable
Than juries whom he handled well.
For firstly, Maud (who, if 'twere known,
Knew nought of her own race) looked down
Upon his humble origin ;
And secondly, she was not in
The best of tempers, seeing Phil,
Whom she thought so adorable,
Wasting attention upon Kit,
Who barely tolerated it.

    Hall talked to Madge, or rather both
Sat by each other and seemed loath
To talk to others.   Last of all,
Miss Ridley would have gone to wall
Had it not been for Kit, who was
The innocent but active cause

Of Phil's ineffable disgust,
For he had meant to have discussed
Matters for Kit's own private ear,
Which she was anxious not to hear,
And, seeing that the governess
Was all alone, began to express
Her pity and invited her
To come and sit down where they were,
Contriving that the talk should be
On subjects to include all three.
Kit really had a gracious heart
And liked to act a friendly part :
But there was truly to confess
One unto whom her kindliness
Would have been much more grateful than
The governess—the gentleman
Who sat on her right hand and gazed
Upon her face till well nigh dazed.

   *   *   *   *

Hall, the Professor, Will and Lil
Had ridden.   Kit so dreaded Phil
That she had given up her horse
To Hall, and driven to the course
Lest any accident should force
The fatal tete-à-tete.   Phil drove,
He was so visibly in love
That when he said he wished to drive
(Which was when he'd heard Kit arrive
At her decision), Will gave up
And rode.   For neither cared to stoop
To th' other's driving which they thought

Uninteresting if not fraught
With ignominy positive,
Having for years been wont to live
Like independent potentates
Of equal, jealous, neighbouring states.
  Kit would not ride upon the box
And play the goose beside the fox
For reasons obvious, and Maud,
For reasons just as plain and broad,
Could not, in justice to her pride,
Take a position by his side,
And Madge knew by experience
How Phil could illustrate his sense
Of being victimised, too well
To think the post desirable,
And Phil could hardly interfere
With Ida, whom the ex-minister
Made in a kind of way his own,
Although he gladly would have done,
For, failing Kit, he liked to be
With Ida, who dressed daintily,
And had the manners of the class
With whom he wished his days to pass.
He was not of a kind to press
Attentions on the governess,
And so he found himself left with
His pet aversion—Lachlan Smith.
To Phil's more educated eye
The barrister's gentility
Was shoddy and suggestive of
A " Monster Outfitting Alcove,"

With his frock-coat not fitting well,
And hat the converse of a bell,
And long shirt cuffs and large breast pin,
And collar forcing up his chin.
    And his pretentious arguings
On races, stock and other things,
Of which he was quite ignorant,
With people who were conversant
Were calculated to confirm
And not remove suspicion's germ.
    But Lachlan Smith talked glibly on
These topics dangerous upon,
The whole way there and whole way back
Without suspecting any lack
Of cordial responsiveness,
Although if he had chattered less
And pondered more he must have seen
Phil's ill-disguised contempt and spleen,
And was so well pleased in his mind
With his success that he inclined
To be almost familiar,
And might have gone a step too far
Had they not fortunately come,
Just as they verged upon it, home.
        *   *   *   *

That being the last night of all,
Even the unæsthetic Hall
Sat down to listen to the tale.
Madge was named Queen without avail,
Insisting that her governess
Was fitter, though when they did press

Miss Ridley she could testify
No more originality
Than timidly to give once more
The subject of the night before—
      Love.

THE SEVEN FAIRIES.

I dreamed a dream of a lady fair,
  A dream of a lady's birth.
There were six fairies assembled there
  From the East and West and North,

All bidden to honour the christening
  In hope of a fairy gift,
But when they answered the fair bidding
  There was yet one fairy left.

Oh ! she lives down in the South, they said,
  Oh, she lives down in the South,
Her face is fair and her cheeks are red,
  But she hath a cruel mouth.

Oh ! she lives down in the South, they said,
  In the halls of ice and snow,
And a breath of her chilling home is shed
  Wherever her footsteps go.

Two fairies came from the golden East,
 And wealth and affection brought,
They came from where jewels the costliest
 Of Golconda's gems are wrought,

From where the sorrowing wife is fain
 To share the funeral throne
With her dead lord rather than remain
 In the lonely world alone.

And two there came from the western lands,
 With brightness of sunny France,
And Tuscan genius in their hands,
 With its tinge of wild romance.

And there were two from the sturdy North,
 And their gifts were homely sense
And glowing health, with generous mirth
 And freedom from false pretence.

And lastly came Envy from the South,
 To offer her offerings,
With her fair cheeks and her cruel mouth,
 And a chill draught from her wings.

But her cruel mouth was wreathed in smiles,
 And soothly "I come," she said,
"From the frozen bounds of Antarctic isles
 My gift unbidden to add.

" You gave her love and you gave her wealth
    And brightness and genius,
You gave her wisdom and gave her health,
    I give her the glorious,

" The peerless crown of beauty to wear
    Her lifelong upon her brow,
And ever in her right hand to bear
    The grace to which all men bow."

And then she opened her draughty wings
    And fled to the realm of ice,
Leaving the child with her offerings
    Of rich and dainty device.

And there rose a hum of glad relief
    That Envy had come and gone
Without a word of anger or grief
    For being the unasked one.

And a glow of transport through them thrilled
    At Envy's glorious gift,
For Envy was vengeful when ill-willed,
    And Envy's revenge was swift.

But amid the glow there came a chill,
    And amid the hum a moan,
And her cold wings seemed to wave there still
    Though she to her home had flown.

And e'en the good fays fell murmuring
  That Envy had outgraced all
In the gift she brought without summoning
  To the christening festival.

II.

The years fled onwards within my dream,
  And with them Desirée grew
Into a form that might well beseem
  The Fairy queen of the dew,

Loving and sensible, healthy, bright,
  With clear intelligent eye
Reflecting the intellect's inward light,
  Reared in all the luxury

Which wealth could pay for and art supply,
  And with every wish fulfilled,
That kindly forethought could satisfy,
  Almost as soon as 'twas willed.

But even the mates of her childish hours
  Had always begrudged her less
Her wealth and health and mind's rare powers,
  Her wisdom and happiness,

Than the crown of beauty that Envy set
  Upon her brow as a gift,

Which seemed in sooth as though it had yet
　　Some taint of the giver left.

III.

The years flew onwards within my dream,
　　Once more Desirée I saw,
A woman such as might well beseem
　　Apelles' pencil to draw ;

Bright as the morning, glowing with health,
　　Warm-hearted tho' worldly wise,
With each allurement added that wealth
　　And art and love could devise,

With a face as beautiful as the day,
　　And a body fairy light,
And upon her a winning grace alway
　　That conquered man's love at sight,

With genius stamped upon the brow
　　And speaking out from her eye,
A queen of love to whom all should bow
　　In homage reverently.

IV.

One day, but no longer in my dream,
　　Came there one his suit to plead,

Wealthy and held in high esteem,
  Of an ancient house the head.

He cared not for wealth, for his own was great,
  He cared not for happy ways,
He cared not for wisdom, nor sought a mate
  For the love which sweetens days.

He loved not the light of genius,
  Or the glowing cheek of health,
And her spirit high and generous
  He valued no more than wealth.

But her peerless beauty grew on him,
  And he hated each arm that stole
In dance or jest round her body slim
  From the depths of his grim soul.

And when he asked her to be his wife,
  And spoke of his wealth and state,
And the gorgeous trappings of his life,
  And his halls of ancient date,

Her mother was dazzled and bade her yield,
  As many a mother before
Has betrayed a child who on foughten field
  Would have held her own in war.

She yielded.   Envy triumphed again
  With her insidious gift,
And on the marriage followed amain
  With feet relentless and swift.

And when any glance or word addressed
  To his graceful, gifted wife,
A blast of envy would pierce his breast
  Like the cutting of a knife.

But he was not the husband for her,
  With her ready sympathy
And fanciful active character
  And warmth of heart and eye.

For she could not but see, with her clear sense,
  How base and poor was the clay
To which she had vowed obedience
  Upon her marriage day,

And she could not dissemble her delight
  When men, with the power of brain
And pride of life that were hers by right,
  To linger by her were fain.

And she so hungered for sympathy
  And appreciative praise,
That perhaps there was too much light in her eye,
  And too much warmth in her ways,

When she heard what she to hear was fain
    From one whose body and mind
Seemed by nature for the praise of men
    And love of women designed.

v.

At last to her husband's Hall by chance
    Came a poet and wanderer,
Rich with the learning of old Romance,
    And a sailer round our sphere.

He spoke of the balmy western isles
    Stretched off the Morocco coast,
And the wondrous glacier-scooped defiles
    That are aye the Switzer's boast.

He spoke of the forests of Brazil,
    And of Canadian woods
When autumn tints are on plain and hill,
    And of mighty falls and floods.

He spoke of spice archipelagos
    And palm-clustered coral reefs,
Round which the smiling Pacific flows,
    And stupendous Austral cliffs,

Of the feudal castles of Norman France.
    The cities of Languedoc,

Of the Vega's green luxuriance,
  And Granada's haunted rock,

Of the fallen monuments of pride
  Set up by the Romans' hand,
Of the grand old town at Arno's side,
  And the burgs of Vaterland,

Of the deathless marbles of antique Greece,
  And the Tajs of Hindustan,
And Egypt's monolith masterpiece,
  And stone-marvels Mexican,

And the gracefullest women of earth,
  The daughters of proud Castile,
Queen slaves of Circassian birth,
  And Greeks with the old profile.

And he whispered that none were so fair
  As she with the grace we so prize,
With the wave of her glittering hair,
  And the gleam of her glorious eyes.

He told her legends of old Romance
  In fable and history,
Of Mary Queen of Scotland and France,
  And Frances of Rimini,

P

Of Guinevere, Grissel and Elaine,
  And the Ysoldes fair and dark,
Sir Tristram's gentle wife-chatelaine,
  And his love, the wife of Marc,

Of Dido the Carthaginian,
  Who for her passion died,
And of the mighty Athenian
  And his Ionian bride,

Of Frithjof and Ingebjorg the queen,
  Of Brynhild and sad Gudrun,
And Sigurd and the last battle scene
  In the palace of the Hun,

Of Henry and fair frail Rosamond,
  And fair chaste Eleanor
Who sucked the venom from Edward's wound,
  Though she should die therefore.

And he whispered that none were so fair
  As she with the grace we so prize,
With the wave of her glittering hair,
  And the gleam of her glorious eyes.

He was goodly enough for her love,
  Had brain enough for her brain,

And it seemed as if Heaven above
  Had meant them for one, not twain.

And with hearts they joined but not with hands,
  Although his indeed were free,
For hers were linked in the fetter-bands
  Of a marriage slavery.

Yet Envy seemed to sleep for a while,
  As if to entice them on
With a subtle cruelty and guile
  For a deeper fall anon.

And her lord so jealous heretofore
  Seemed to doze in apathy,
While she was carried out more and more
  On to the enchanted sea

Of love for an object worthy of love,
  Of love that would elevate,
If Fancy only were free to rove
  In her original state.

And Envy slept until they should come
  Into their fool's paradise
Of the intercourse which lights a home
  With pure and rational joys.

And then she awoke and struck her dart
  So deeply into the side
Of the jealous husband, that his heart
  Was choked with the surging tide
Of passion and hatred, which did start,
  And without one word he died.

vi.

Alas for Desirée, wooed and won
  By the husband now of her choice,
For Envy's spite still made her its own,
  And held her as in a vice.

For her tyrant's swift mysterious death
  And her speedy union
Aroused Report's calumnious breath,
  And estranged friends one by one.

Alas for Desirée, though she had wealth
  And brightness and genius,
And mellow wisdom and glowing health,
  Though she had the glorious,

The peerless crown of beauty to wear
  Her lifelong upon her brow,
And ever in her right hand to bear
  The grace to which all men bow,

Though she had the husband whom she chose,
　Though her hands at length were free
From the fetter-bands so cruelly close
　Of her marriage slavery,

She could not live in the land of her love,
　The land of her broad estates,
But ever away from home must rove
　Impelled by pitiless fates.

And so they came to a far-off isle
　On the lone Pacific's breast,
And here they live in repose awhile,
　Even Envy letting them rest.

And here this beautiful English dame
　And brilliant Englishman,
With their broad estates and ancient name
　Unsullied by real stain,

Live in soft exile, and never see
　The face of their countrymen,
Save when a schooner from Sydney quay
　Sails down with their stores, and then
Only some mariner rough and free
　Who finds them beyond his ken—

This delicate dame in soft attire,
　　With wondrous beauty of face,
And white wise forehead and glance of fire,
　　And unforgettable grace,

This lordly man of wealth without bound,
　　And rich in knowledge and worth,
Thus living as one might say beyond
　　The uttermost end of earth.

Adieu, Desirée, living thus far,
　　A kind of enchanted queen
To mariners when they cross the bar
　　Of your harbour coraline !

Mayhap it may prove a magic isle
　　Where Envy shall not prevail
To banish your pleasure with her guile
　　And peace with her icy gale.

Those whom the powers would have destroyed
They make of understanding void.
Phil, when at length the tale was o'er,
Proposed to have a dance once more,
And Kit, well pleased with her success
Of last night, was in readiness
To dance again, because she thought
This course with less of danger fraught,

And one who danced so perfectly
Needs must enjoy Phil's mastery
Of step and poise : and so she danced
Dance after dance, herself entranced
With his facility, and he
With her new affability.
Not only did she thus deceive
Herself, but made them all believe
That she relented.   She was fair
Enough to make a man despair,
And rosy-cheeked with golden curl
Cut short, not so much like a girl
As like a lovely, glowing boy
Ere manhood hastens to destroy
The silky smoothness of his face,
Only that they have scant of grace
And she so much.   In height she stood
Above the mean of womanhood,
But not unduly.   She was slim,
As Australs are, of waist, and limb
At wrist and ankle, but more full
Up higher.   Lithe and powerful
As health and constant exercise
Could make her, with her clear grey eyes,
Symbolic of her proud, brave soul,
A woman taken as a whole,
In her sole self embodying
All which makes man creation's king,
And woman its chief ornament.
No wonder then that all eyes bent
On her as she waltzed lightly by

With glowing cheek and sparkling eye
And ruffled curls, surrendering
Her motions to Phil's piloting
Without remonstrance, and thereby
Filling the grand deficiency
Which left her beauty incomplete,
That which makes maidenhood as sweet
As a moss-rose or violet,
Or the green grass of spring, ere yet
It feels the cruel searing stress
Of summer—maiden gentleness.
    It is not easy to maintain
An attitude of cold disdain
When one is heated with a dance,
And Kit relaxed her vigilance
So far as to be cordial
To Phil's oft ineffectual
But still repeated courtesies,
So much so that he deemed his prize
Within his grasp, and suddenly
Waltzing her almost forcibly
Into the open boudoir, closed
The door behind him—and proposed.
    Kit was so thunderstruck that he
Had kissed her twice triumphantly
Ere she gave her indignant ' no,'
And then fierce tears began to flow
At the humiliating state
In which she found herself—irate
First with herself for being caught
In her own trap, then with Phil Forte

For having dared to offer her
Such ignominy, angrier
When she reflected how her mien
Must have encouraged him that e'en,
Yet did not hurry to the door
Now that the worst of it was o'er,
But stayed a little while to vent
Her anger and astonishment,
And to compose her countenance
Before she went back to the dance.
   " How dare you, Phil?" she said at length,
When her mind had regained its strength,
" How dare you?" but then, seeing how
He was prostrated by the blow,
Her good heart triumphed and she said,
Lifting her gallant, graceful head
To look at him with firm, pained eyes,
" Phil, was it right or kind or wise
To take advantage of me thus?
I thought you were more generous,
Than to abuse my confidence,
Knowing, as you well do, the sense
Of loathing for the marriage-bond
I entertain.   Were you as fond
Of me as you pretend you are,
You'd banish all such thoughts afar
And treat me as a brother, Phil,
In fact just like your brother Will."
   "You like him better.   I have seen
Him kissing you—you . . ." " Why," we've been
Neighbours and friends this twenty years,

And I'd do more than box his ears
Unless I knew that it was done
Merely to tease me—just his fun.
No, Phil.   I do not love him more
But like him better, as before
You persecuted, I liked you,
And as I still should like you too
If you were fond enough of me
Not to tease me so cruelly."
"Cruelly, Kit?   It's not unkind
To love with one's whole heart and mind."
"Love? what is there in me to love?"
"To love in you, who are above
All women in all graces which
The lot of womanhood enrich."
"There's hardly any girl you meet
Who's not more graceful and more sweet."
"O Kit, you cannot be so dull
As not to know how beautiful,
How graceful, how superb, how far
Above the common herd you are."
"Phil, this is flattery, don't try
Me with mere compliments to buy."
"Kit," he said so reproachfully,
That she went up with softened eye,
And putting her two hands in his,
Said, "Well then, Phil, give me a kiss,
And promise never to refer
To this unpleasant rencontre,
And not to speak to me again
Of marriage.   Then we can remain

Friends as before.   I will not be
An atom different, and we
Can easily keep out of sight
All that has happened here to-night,
Otherwise I must go away
To-morrow early in the day."
　　He did not take the proffered kiss,
But shook his head.   "I can't do this :
I can but love you all my life,
And pray you to become my wife
Whenever chance lets me intrude
Upon you in a generous mood."
　　"Well then, good-bye, Phil ! take me back,
I'll say that I feel an attack
Of headache coming over me
And bid them good-night hurriedly.
　　　　*　　　*　　　*　　　*
Kit went to bed, and Phil went out
To walk with rapid stride about,
In hopes of working off his load
Of disappointed love, and strode
Till long past midnight.   The next day
Kit packed her 'traps' and drove away
Back to her father's place, which lay
Some twenty miles off.   Phil went up,
Meaning, for the first time, to stop
Some months upon his Queensland run.
Chesterfield took Maud Morrison
And Ida Lewis back to town,
Hall, Phil Forte's partner, just stayed down
To do some station-business,

Which Phil, who posted off express,
Left pending.   Lachlan Smith ere long
Went, for assize-work, to Geelong.

      *   *   *   *

Two months were left ere term began,
And one of them like lightning ran
In wandering about with Lil,
And sometimes driving out with Will
All over pleasant Waratah
And stations that were not too far.
   Then the Professor had to leave
To make his home fit to receive
Its pretty mistress (for the day
Was fixed, long ere he went away,
To be some three weeks' space before
The long vacation time was o'er).
And Lil, the day that he went back,
Went to their own house in Toorak
With Mrs Forte, to help to choose
The furniture she was to use,
Her father's wedding gift.   He gave
Carte blanche to both of them to have
Whatever they thought requisite
To deck their house or furnish it.
Three weeks thus busy quickly passed,
Then Lil went back to spend her last
At home, while the Professor stayed,
And final preparations made
For their reception.   For they meant
(And persevered in their intent)
To have their honeymoon at home

In their own house, and not to roam
In boarding-houses and hotels
As they saw everybody else,
Affording people food for jest
Or food for pity at the best.
How much more sensible it is
In ordinary marriages
Where the bridegroom has not too much
Of time or money in his clutch,
To spend the little that he has
In adding those etceteras
Which go to make a little house
Dainty if not luxurious.
Much honeymoonshine in home life
Is not the lot of every wife,
And so the golden month should be
Economised most carefully
In gilding every room and nook,
A flower-bed here, and there a book,
With one of the small sorceries
So magical in lovers' eyes.
Ah, pitiful ! there's many a home
To which no love-making has come,
Passion's brief transport being spent
Ere they into its portals went,
The man a business-machine,
The woman not her husband's queen
But his housekeeper—and here judge
If I speak truth or not—his drudge.
Newly-wed lovers should not roam,
But stay to beautify their home

With blossoms of the honeymoon,
' So hard to mimic when it's gone.
    The weary reader will not care
To go to the upholsterer
With Lil to see how the refined
And graceful tenour of her mind
Declared itself in ottomans,
Or took an airy flight in fans,
But be content to leave her here
In the enchanted atmosphere
Of trysting days,—a maiden fair
Without the shadow of a care
To keep back from her passion-flower
The full spring-sunshine of its hour.

Finished at SPRINGWOOD,
        BLUE MOUNTAINS,
            NEW SOUTH WALES.

1.7 A.M., *September* 17*th*, 1883.

UPON THE S.S. "BALLAARAT," *

Off Ushant, *May 25th*, 1884.

(Dedicated to the Hon. J. B. WATT of Sydney.)

O stately ship, fast-speeding to thy port,
  Our home for six bright weeks of sunny weather,
  We have had many pleasant hours together
Since we embarked—voyagers of either sort,
Old colonists returning to the land
  They left long since to win an independence,
  And young folks, born Australians, in attendance,
Longing to see their Father's native strand.
  We shall not leave our ship without a sigh,
    In which were born so many loves, hopes, fears,
    And friendships sure to last for many years,
Or the blithe officers who brought us by
    Australia, Asia, Africa, to rest
    Safe in our dear old island of the West.

* A P. and O. Steamer.

Opinions of the Press

ON WORKS BY THE SAME AUTHOR.

———◆———

"FRITHJOF AND INGEBJORG,"

AND OTHER POEMS.

BY AN AUSTRALIAN COLONIST.

London: C. Kegan Paul, Trench, & Co.

Of "Frithjof and Ingebjorg" the Argus, writing in the fall of 1881, says :—

"A further instalment of Mr Sladen's metrical version of a saga of 'Frithjoff and Ingebjorg' confirms the favourable opinion we expressed of the first part. It is so good both in form and substance as to justify the expectation that the writer will hereafter make his mark in the poetical literature of Australia."

From the Age *and* Leader, *October* 1882.

The ode to Somnus reveals in form the influence of Keats, and, despite its not unnatural prosiness, Wiltshire has a ring of the Wordsworthian metal. In his epilogue, however, Mr Sladen makes his confession of poetical faith, and announces himself a disciple of Longfellow, whom he certainly resembles in his range of subjects. His rendering of Virgil's "Tenth Eclogue" has a flow that reminds one of "Evangeline." One of the best of his lyrics is "L'Ordre de Bel Eyse"—

"First we love fair ladies,   These are to divert us,
Then we love good books;   Those are to entice us ;
Either have their virtues,   Books outlive their pages,
Either have their vices ;   Ladies their good looks."

But decidedly his best effort, and the only poem in which he has kept a sustained level of excellence, is that from which his collection takes its title, "Frithjof and Ingebjorg." The legend is treated with artistic feeling, and the verse flows smoothly and sweetly throughout. One might even say that it proves its author to be a worthy scholar of the master who gave us the "Tales of a Wayside Inn," and express a hope that he may never fall below this achievement in future.

From the FEDERAL AUSTRALIAN, October 19th, 1882.

Mr D. B. W. Sladen is already favourably known to Australian readers, several of the poems in this handsome little volume having been previously published in the "Victorian Review," and to many their reprint will be welcome. We have read the volume with pleasure, and gladly bring it under the notice of our readers, not only because it is the work of a colonist, but also because it contains much that is really good, and holds out the promise of some better work in the future. In his "epilogue" the author writes thus modestly :—

> "Australia sends this book of song
>   To England, not so much in hope
> That it will take its place among
>   The brotherhood of wider scope,
> But rather that it will be read
>   By those who take this volume up
> Remembering where it was bred.
>   We cannot, in our youth, compare
> With the full-grown and perfected
>   Poesy reared in English air."

And then, further on :—

> "Where this small sheaf of rhyme did grow,
>   We have not yet lived fifty years :
> But as the swift hours onward flow,
>   We too shall breed poetic peers
> For Arnold and for Tennyson ;
>   And, without vanity or fears,
> Not shrink from competition
>   With Bryant, Whittier, and the rest
> Who've made their country's lyre known
>   To Anglo-Saxon, east and west."

Such are Mr Sladen's high hopes, and we doubt not their realization in the not far distant future.

The poems in this volume are on a great variety of themes—grave and gay. Most readers will probably consider the well-told story of "Frithjof and Ingebjorg" the best in many respects ; but a considerable number of the shorter poems are interesting, and contain many fine lines. We name specially "St Paul at Athens," founded on the historic narrative in the Book of the Acts of the Apostles, xvii. 16-34, "The Last of the Vikings," which carries us back to the days of the Saxon Harold. Among the short poems we may also name "The Dead Old Year," "The Voyage of Life," and "On a New-born Babe," all of which contain many beautiful thoughts.

The volume is beautifully printed, and, we hope, will be favourably received, and find a place in many a home library.

Q

From the S. A. REGISTER, *and* ADELAIDE OBSERVER, *October* 1882.

Of these, "Frithjof and Ingebjorg," a Norwegian legend, written in an attempt at the old rugged style of the saga, is perhaps the best. It is too long to quote, but not too lengthy to read. There are some original ideas in it, and the language in which it is clothed is poetical. The "Squire's Brother" is also a piece in which the author has shown originality of thought, as well as skill in working out.

From the QUEENSLANDER, *December* 23rd, 1882.

The title of Mr Douglas B. W. Sladen's book is, to our Southern ears, the least musical portion of it ; but before the poem "Frithjof and Ingebjorg" has been fully perused, the reader will probably have forgotten the title and become absorbed in the romantic story cleverly woven into verse. Those who have read occasionally-published lines by Mr Sladen will doubtless look for good and scholarly work in his compilation. They will be by no means disappointed, for the principal items have in them a true poetic ring, and no suspicion of crudeness. The publication is not, however, what might be termed even. In some of the lesser poems everything seems to have been sacrificed to simplicity, and one or two of the pieces produced, such as those commencing—

> " Oft in the noon of even
> When I am in my bed,"

and the fourth verse of "Westward Ho!" seem scarcely worthy of Mr Sladen's pen, unless, indeed, they were scribbled off in some moment of inspiration which could not find proper expression ; and, if that be so, they would have been better not published in companionship with such lines as "Waterloo," "Sappho," "Roman Cirencester," and "the Last of the Britons."

In "Waterloo" there is a facility of rhythm which we miss in almost every other poem. It is written in a fine inspiriting strain, such so lifts the reader up, until, to use Shelley's words—

> " The dead air seems alive
> With the clash of clanging wheels
> And the tramp of horses' heels."

The lines are pretty well known to those who take an interest in the new literature of the colonies, and have passed from journal to journal in our small literary world with almost the same universal publication as did "Hands all Round," but with far better appreciation. There is a joyous ring in the lines—

> "On, on,
> Life Guard and Dragoon,
> ' An English charge and a red right hand
> Will bring fair years to your fair old land.
> With riven corslet and shivered lance
> Is reft and shivered the pride of France."

And, again, there is a charming expression in the concluding verse—

> " 'Ah! me,
> Life is sad,' said she,
> 'When the sun and sheen of it are gone,'
> And 'One loving heart is very lone;'
> And 'Oh! if I might lie by you
> In your soldier grave at Waterloo.' "

The poetry of Mr Sladen, as judged by his book, seems well described in the following from Thomson's " Winter "—

> " O'er the sanded valley floating spreads,
> Calm, sluggish, silent till again constrained
> Betwixt two meeting hills it bursts away."

The production of what we term the uninteresting and uninterestingly told personal emotions of the poet does not detract from his merit or claim to be enrolled among those who are destined to reach the heights of Olympus and share the joys of the eternal spring. There are many who look with astonishment on some of the published poetry of Tennyson, but who will deny the possession of the Divine afflatus to the author of " Enoch Arden," the " Charge of the Light Brigade," and other verse which is known wherever the Anglo-Saxon tongue is spoken, or translations can bear their beauty and vigour? In telling the story of " Frithjof and Ingebjorg," Mr Sladen has followed a course which characterises Moore's " Lalla Rookh." He has given us a very improbable romance but so cunningly draped in soft poetic expression as to be acceptable even to those who like hard facts plainly told. If one could not hope for such a happy realisation of the fates of the hero and heroine as the poem gives us, so well are the human sympathies attacked that a wish at all events would accord with the author's working out of the plot. " Sappho " is a better poem perhaps, and in " Ravenna " there is a scholarly form of expression which seems to show itself in all the writing of men who have given much study to the classic literature of Rome. The book, on the whole, is an acquisition to Australian poetic literature of which no colonist need feel ashamed—they may feel proud of the purity of thought and expression which alone would recommend it, and give it a place where more stirring and less pure works would be denied.

From the Scotsman (*Edinburgh*), *November* 30*th*, 1882.

A volume of simple, easy, flowing verse, so writ that all who run may read and understand, is Mr Sladen's " Frithjof and Ingebjorg." Mr Sladen announces himself on his title-page as " an Australian colonist," and many of his poems are on themes connected with his voluntary exile, its pleasures and its penalties, loving recollections of the old country, hope and pride in the new one. Then he has pleasant lyrics and ballads, songs of the affections, and fragments on subjects borrowed from classic story. All alike are characterised by a satisfying mastery of form and metre, a clearness and directness of style in wholesome contrast to the morbid mysticism which pervades so much the poetry of the day, breadth and elevation of thought, and a genuine appreciation of the true and the beautiful. There is nothing in the volume that the reader could readily spare ; there is much that will be read again and again with hearty enjoyment.

THE GRAPHIC, *November*, 1882.

There is some good verse in " Frithjof and Ingebjorg, and other Poems," by Douglas B. W. Sladen (Kegan Paul). The author, now resident in Australia, and apparently an *alumnus* of Rugby, has something of the true poetic feeling ; it seems a pity that he has not more fully developed the vein of innate humour manifested in "My Aunt." In the principal piece he probably depended upon translations—which are, without exception, as 'bad as they well could be—for there is nothing to show any real knowledge of or sympathy with Scandinavian lore. "The Squire's Brother" is good, with a natural pathos; "The Last of the Britons" also has merit.

The GLASGOW HERALD, *December* 2, 1882.

In the epilogue to this little collection of poems the author pleads thus for a kindly hearing :—

> " Australia sends this book of song
>   To England, not so much in hope
> That it will take its place among
>   The Brotherhood of wider scope,
> But rather that it will be read
>   By those who take this volume up,
> Remembering where it was bred.
>
> You must not judge this book of rhyme
>   By standard of the full-grown muse
> Of our good Queen Victoria's time,
>   But first in dusty tomes peruse
> The rude verse of King Edward's reign,
>   When English first came into use."

The pleading is so graceful that we are glad Mr Sladen has added it ; but there is so much beauty both of thought and language in his poems that they require no advocacy. The chief poem, which gives its name to the collection, is founded upon an old Norse Saga, some passages of which have been translated by Longfellow. But Mr Sladen is no translator. He has taken the story, and, putting it into flowing and musical verse, has shown us lovely pictures of crag and forest, blossom and bush. These are so closely entwined, one with the other, that it is not possible to separate them for quotation. Still less can we pick out any of those passages which tell in a very noble way of the struggles of the two lovers against almost overwhelming temptation ; or of the unselfish love of the aged king for his fair

young bride. Even in the rough hexameters of the American poet the
story is full of pathos and dignity ; but when wedded to Mr Sladen's tender
and musical words, it must charm all who read it. Besides " Frithjof,"
there are several other long poems, which contain many beautiful passages,
and there are a number of shorter pieces. Of these, " Waterloo" and
" Wiltshire " are pathetic and suggestive. but they are too long for quotation.
We prefer to give a few verses of "The Squire's Brother." The elder
brother is " squire," the younger goes to Australia where he works

> " Harder than any labourer
> Upon my brother's lands,"

and wonders what ' Nell ' would think of him, did she see him, once the
' Cupid' forte of ' White's,'

> " Lolling in a linen blouse,
> And bearded to the brow."

He then goes on—

> " Do you suppose that old Sir Hugh,
> Who won your lands in mail,
> Showed half the valour that I do
> In sitting on this rail?
> He tilted in his lordly way,
> And stoutly, I confess,
> But I stand sentry all the day
> Against the wilderness.
> There isn't much poetical
> About an old tweed suit,
> And nothing chivalrous at all
> About a cowhide boot :
> Yet often beneath a bushman's breast
> There lurks a knightly soul,
> And bushmen's feet have often pressed
> Towards a gallant goal.
> And so I slave and stay and save,
> And squander nought but youth ;
> And if Nell said that I was brave,
> She only told the truth."

From the WESTMINSTER REVIEW, *January* 1883.

In his modest and not unpleasing epilogue to " Frithjof and Ingebjorg
and other Poems," Mr Douglas B. W. Sladen tells us that he writes from
Australia, that he desires to follow in the footsteps of Mr Longfellow, and
would be judged by the humble if somewhat obscure standard of

> " What the American
> Could write two centuries ago."

We read with pleasure the tale of " Frithjof and Ingebjorg," and can recommend it to our readers. A good tale well told justifies publication.

From the CHELTONIAN, *November*, 1882.

We gladly welcome " Frithjof and Ingebjorg and other Poems," by a well-known O.C., formerly Editor of the "Cheltonian," Captain of the Football Team and of the Rifle Corps, now "an Australian Colonist"—D. B. W. Sladen, B.A., late Scholar of Trinity College, Oxford. Several of the pieces have appeared in the "Australasian" and the "Queenslander" ; a few in our own pages at various times. The longer poem that gives its name to the volume has many striking passages, but we like some of the shorter pieces better. The common sense of the following would have done Kingsley's heart good :

> " But you cannot expect a man to speak
>   In the true poetic way
> Of spots where he gets ten shillings a week
>   And works twelve hours a day."

We can heartily recommend the volume to our readers. It is published by Messrs Kegan Paul, Trench & Co.

AUSTRALIAN LYRICS.

London : GRIFFITH & FARRAN, St Paul's Churchyard, E.C.

GEORGE ROBERTSON, Sydney, Melbourne, and Adelaide.

From the ARGUS, *March 5th,* 1883.

In a brief preface to Australian Lyrics, Mr D. B. W. Sladen mentions that "every poem in the book has passed the ordeal of editorial criticism into one or other of the leading metropolitan journals of Australia," so that it is unnecessary to do more than call attention to the fact that they have been collected into a handsomely printed brochure, with that breadth of margin, clearness of type, and smoothness of paper, which are calculated to render them still more acceptable to the reader.

From the LEADER, *March* 3, 1882.

This collection of Australian Lyrics will be welcome to all who have read Mr Sladen's Norwegian Saga. Although these later poems have been written with unusual celerity, presuming that they have been all written since the publication of his previous poetic efforts ; yet they show no falling off in regard to poetic power, and are entitled to be received with no less favour. A line here and there may be detected as wanting in smoothness, but upon the whole, the verses show a mastery of form and metre, and a sweetness of flow that is pleasant to the ear. A charming simplicity both of expression and of idea, is their prominent characteristic, as might be expected of one who can say of Longfellow—

> " Was not his simple song
> Our sample of all song ? "

The collection is not without variety, although the writer has evidently a predilection for certain themes, and in regard to these is apt to repeat himself. The themes to which he most frequently recurs are those which enable him to sing of home and family affections, of fair women and love's young dream, and to indulge in regrets for having left Old England even for " the blue of Austral skies."

The divided feeling with which Mr Sladen regards his old home and the new is fairly exhibited in " The Squire's Brother," the longest in the collection, and, in our opinion, the best of the lot. In the first part the Squire's Brother, who is a younger son and who has been sent out to Queensland to push his fortune as a squatter, soliloquises as he sits on a three-rail fence—

> " Nell wouldn't know me, I suppose, were she to see me now
> Thus lolling in a linen blouse and bearded to the brow ;
> I didn't wear a flannel shirt when I was courting her,
> Or buck-skin pants engrained with dirt and shiny as a spur.

So here I am—a pioneer, working with my own hands
Harder than any labourer upon my brother's lands,
Far from the haunts of gentlemen in this outlandish place ;
I wonder if I e'er again shall see a woman's face.

I couldn't stand it, but for this, that when I first came out,
I used to see the carriages in which men drove about,
Who tended sheep themselves of old 'neath Caledonia's rocks,
And now were lords of wealth untold, and half a hundred flocks.

I laid this unction to my heart, that, if a Scottish hind
Could play so manfully his part, I should not be behind:
And so I slave and stay and save, and squander nought but youth ;
Nell sometimes writes and calls me brave, and knows but half the truth."

Part second takes us to the old hall, where we see the returned squatter gazing at the family portraits on the walls—

"The photo in the frame is Nell—why I gave Dick that frame,
And doesn't the old pet look well ! I swear she's just the same
As when I left her years ago to cross the Southern foam,
I wonder if they've let her know that I'm expected home."

Part third introduces us to Nellie herself, standing " before a faded carte," and thus soliloquising in her turn after having seen her old lover—

" But Charlie's very different, he's seen the real world,
And where no white man ever went his lonely flag unfurled ;
He went to slave and stay and save and squander nothing but youth,
And when I said that he was brave I knew but half the truth.

For there in intermittent strife, with hostile natives waged
He spent the best years of his life in humdrum toil engaged,
Or galloping the live long day under a Queensland sun
After some bullocks gone astray or stolen off the run.

He's handsomer, I think, to-day, although he is so brown,
And though his hair is tinged with grey and thin upon the crown,
Than in the days when he was known at " White's " as Cupid Forte,
And in good looks could hold his own with any man at court,

Well, he has come and asked again that which he came to ask
The night before he crossed the main upon his uphill task.
I answer'd as I answer'd then but with a lighter heart.
Who knew if we should meet again the day we had to part ! "

And then in the fourth and concluding part we have one of those dainty pictures which Mr Sladen paints so deftly with a few touches of his pen—a picture of Charlie and Nellie in the first flush of married life—

" 'Neath a verandah in Toorak I sit this summer morn,
While from the garden at the back, upon the breezes borne,
There floats a subtle, faint perfume of oleander bow'rs
And broad magnolias in bloom, and opening orange flow'rs,

A lady 'mid the flowers I see, moving with footsteps light,
And when she stoops she shows to me a slipper slim and bright,
An ankle stocking'd in black silk and rounded as a palm,
Her dress is of the hue of milk and making of madame.

I wonder is that garden hat intended to conceal
All but that heavy auburn plait, or merely to reveal
Enough to make one long to catch a glimpse of what is there,
To see if eye and feature match the glory of the hair."

Extract from a Letter to the Editor of the OTAGO DAILY TIMES,
Dunedin, N.Z., published in that paper.

Now, Sir, I do not wish to imply that the critic who reviewed Mr
Sladen's book in your columns is not possessed of all the attributes which
go to form the character of a poetical analyst; but I maintain that the
element of fair play appears to be strange to him. He has picked out all
the weeds from the work, and has failed to exhibit to your readers any of
its flowers. I have not yet had the necessary time at my disposal to read
the book through, but from the fact that Mr Sladen is a contributor to the
"Victorian Review" and other leading periodicals, I am led to hope that
there are a number of literary buds among his "Australian Lyrics," and
that your critic has only picked out the dead leaves. Opening the book at
random, my eyes fell on an effusion headed "Wiltshire," and as your
reviewer was pretty severe on it, I was induced to run it through. The
perusal of the poem confirms me in my belief that your critic has not dealt
fairly with Mr Sladen. The object of the verses is to prove that country
life is more suited to children than city life. Your critic in quoting one
verse, and that the worst in the poem, observes—
In the poem called "Wiltshire" this imaginative verse occurs:—

> "But when they summon'd up courage to speak,
>   'We hate the country,' they said;
> 'Father used to get ten shillings a week,
>   And now gets thirty instead.
> He used to come back in the evening late,
>   And go off so very soon;
> And now his work doesn't begin till eight,
>   And stops in the afternoon.'"

Beyond rhyme, we venture to say that there are no elements of poetry
about this verse, and it would be much better if Mr Sladen expressed his
views in prose.
May I enquire why he did not quote the following lines from the same
poem—

> "The hedges are surely the place for buds,
>   The meadows for open flowers;
> Little birds should sing away in the woods,
>   In the merry morning hours;

Little children should grow, as the young trees grow,
  Under the sun and the sky,
And their songs should go up, as birds' songs go,
  That hover and sing on high."

In conclusion, sir, allow me to express an opinion that while newspaper critics should discourage the publication of volumes of verse which betray a sterility of imagination and an "impotence of articulation," they should do their utmost to foster colonial literature by bestowing encouragement on young writers who give evidence of the possession of talent which only requires to be matured by time and experience. Iam, etc.,

THOMAS BRACKEN.

From the FEDERAL AUSTRALIAN, *March 29th,* 1883.

Mr Sladen's new volume in its parchment binding is about as pretty a specimen of an edition *de luxe* as has ever yet issued from the Australian press. The poems collected in it have been, for the most part, printed already in the pages of Australian journals, and they are all in lyrical form. In some cases the author rises to a high level of sustained conception and expression; but it must be added, this is rather the exception than the rule. Mr Sladen has the fault natural to all young poets of too great facility and redundancy. He does not follow the wise Voltarian rule to take time that he may be shorter. Were he to use "the labour of the file" more freely his verses would doubtless show a very great improvement in point of thought and language. There are gleams and flashes of the higher faculty observable in them here and there, but the excess of verbiage obscures the bright play of fancy; and—unpardonable in poetry—the verse is spoiled by an unutterably bad rhyme. Thus to rhyme "train her" with "Diana," is totally out of all poetical license. On this point Tennyson has always been exquisitely perfect. There is not now a defective, or faulty, or cockney rhyme to be found in all his works, although his first volume contained some slips of this kind, which were mercilessly dealt with by the critics. When Mr Sladen comes to republish his early effusions, he must, like his master, omit a great deal and amend a great deal. We observe that he, too, has his spiteful and ill-natured critics. He will turn their weapons against themselves by quietly accepting their unkindly comments, and turning them to account. Most of the themes dealt with in the volumes are eminently capable of poetical treatment; but the suggestion continually recurs to the mind of the reader, that the poet could have done better if he had taken greater pains. These suggestions we offer with all good feeling to Mr Sladen. He has it in him to become an Australian Longfellow; but in order to attain this pitch of eminence, he must become as painstaking and artistic a worker as was the author of the "Voices of the Night."

From the MELBOURNE REVIEW, *April,* 1883.

However in spite of the many, the very many blemishes, which mar the book, there is here and there something to praise. The ode to Queen

Victoria is distinctly good, and pleases the student of Horace by an agreeable echo of that wonderful master.

From the GRAPHIC, *July 20th*, 1883.

A true note of song is sounded from the Antipodes in "Australian Lyrics" by Douglas B. W. Sladen (George Robertson, Melbourne, Sydney, and Adelaide). The pieces have all, it seems, appeared in the columns of the Colonial press, and we can only say that any editor was lucky who could secure such a contributor of verse. The best thing in the volume—which, by the bye is of a most uncomfortable shape—is undoubtedly "the Squire's Brother," a tale of true love told in ringing measure, but there is much more that will delight the lover of genuine poetry. "Mrs Watson" is an excellent tribute to the memory of a brave, good woman, and "Solomon's Prayer" is terse and effective. Altogether Mr Sladen's muse is one worthy of being cultivated.

From the ARGONAUT (*San Fransisco*), *April 28th*, 1883.

"Australian Lyrics" is a volume of verse by Douglas B. W. Sladen, B.A. Oxon., of Melbourne, who has already attracted considerable attention by "Frithjof and Ingebjorg," a Scandinavian legend, and is also a regular contributor to the "Victorian Review" and other Australian periodicals. Mr Sladen delights in odd rhymes, and endeavours to preserve as much as possible the natural element in his poems.

From the CUMBERLAND MERCURY, *Saturday, April 7th*, 1883.

The task of the Australian lyrical poet is a difficult one. The sphere in which he must work is naturally contracted. Where there is but a scant stock of national associations—and as yet the purely Australian stock is necessarily limited—there can be but few distinctly Australian songs (other than those which treat either objectively or subjectively of Australian scenery) since the song of a nation is the ultimate test of the national popular spirit. In Australia yet awhile the popular spirit is still, as a rule, British—often flecked and marred by the sordid utilitarianism of the "Manchester School" of thought; hence the ideal situation is peculiarly adverse to Art, whether the art of painter or sweet singer.

By a few members of a limited circle, Australian art-culture is sought after and encouraged; but, outside of that circle, the atmosphere, unfortunately, is more favourable to the positive retardation than to any development, however indirect, of ideality. In Kendall, in Charles Harpur, and in Adam Lindsay Gordon, Australia found true and loyal interpreters of many of her moods and conditions. Their best pieces are as essentially Australian as Burns' best are Scotch or Campbell's British. And other names might be mentioned, of men, ay! and of women too, who have occasionally offered at the shrine of the Muse of Australia a song worthy of "the sweet voice so full with the music of fountains."

Of what weight and consistency are Mr Sladen's claims to be ranked as an Australian lyrical poet? We would say that Mr Sladen's claims rest on a fairly firm basis. He has an Australian way of looking at things. Though not as essentially Australian in his moods as was Kendall, he possesses the power not only of painting local scenery with most graphic touch, but of treating foreign subjects from a distinctly Australian standpoint. The volume before us supplies many proofs of the truth of our assertion. The lyrics it contains are not all of equal merit: indeed the difference between the best and the "least best" is very marked: yet they all reveal a sprightly fancy and a healthy intelligence. There is no passage in them which suggest indifference to pure morality. They have no flavour of morbidity or cynicism: and each whispers a message "adequate to humanity at its best."

Wordsworth-like Mr Sladen evidently believes that it is the singer's mission "to console the afflicted, and to add sunshine to daylight by making the happy happier"; and he has been dowered with the needful powers to practise his belief with both graciousness and efficacy. Not that there are no shortcomings in his work. Mr Sladen's worst fault is a care-lessness with regard to final sounds.

On the other hand, the beauties of Mr Sladen's Lyrics, which brim over with naturalness, are many and great. Here, for instance, is a delightful piece, a true poem—the last stanza whereof strikes us as being a most vivid bit of word-painting :—

OUT WEST IN QUEENSLAND.

" Coifi, the priest of King Edwin, likened the life of man
To the coming of a sparrow, with snow and stormwind wan,
Out of the frost and the darkness into the warmth and light
Of the great hall of the King's house upon a wassail-night.

And after a moment's sojourn, type of the life of men,
Into the frost and darkness fluttering out again.
We sprang from the womb of darkness, and she takes back her own,
And who knoweth whence we issued, or whither we have gone?

Like the brief flight of a sparrow upon a wintry night,
Out of the frost and the darkness into the warmth and light,
Is the advent of a stranger in the back blocks out west,
Here to-night and gone to-morrow, after food, roof, and rest.

Just riding up to the homestead upon a tired horse,
And asking for a night's lodging that's granted as of course :
A shaking of hands and supper, a smoke, a yarn, and bed—
Then saddle and ere the sun's up, the guest has gone, Godsped."

Or take the following "In Memoriam" lines ; what a bright dash of Australian colouring is thrown into the middle stanza (though perhaps the word "meadows" is not quite appropriate)—

IN MEMORIAM : C. Le F.

Born at Grasmere, emigrated to Australia, killed in Afghanistan.

" Wandering over the Cumbrian mountains,
　Herding his flocks on Helvellyn's breast,
Watering sheep at the hill-side fountains,
　The high young spirit could find no rest.

Galloping over Australian meadows
　On the fierce steed that he loved the best,
Only the flickering gum-tree shadows
　'Twixt him and the sun, yet he found no rest.

Under the sky on the Afghan mountains,
　With a foeman's bullet in his breast,
Dead for a draught of the hill-side fountains
　To quench his fever—he lies at rest."

"The Squire's Brother," the longest flight in the volume, is really charming, somewhat Praed-like but thoroughly Australian : the hero being one who in the heat and burden of Queensland's time of small things had "stood sentry all the day against the wilderness," and thereby won affluence and, what he prized more, the possession of the dear English maiden whose heart be had won ere he dared the perils of the bush.

"A Moss Rose of Erin" might have been written by Dante G. Rossetti, in one of whose many styles it is unmistakably cast.

" To the Australian Eleven" is an example of the writer's skill in fun and punning, good enough in its way, yet hardly worthy of a place beside his " Ambition" and his "Nellie," the latter of which pieces, a specimen of the tender way in which Mr Sladen can touch the minor key of sympathy with sorrow, we subjoin as the last of our extracts from his "Australian Lyrics":—

NELLIE (AGED NINE).

" WEEP NOT !
　Call her not dead. She was only nine years old ;
　Her hair was like a cataract all of gold ;
　Faced was she like the cherubim from the first,
　Perchance as a foretoken that she would burst
　　The bonds that held her down from heaven ere long.
　She left off singing in her life's matin-song.
　Weep not !

WEEP NOT !
　She passed from one to another happy home :
　Her little feet had not the leisure to roam
　Off the footpath into the brambles of life;
　She had no time to taste the sorrow and strife
　That damp and mildew and rust a woman's years,
　With schoolgirl's and lover's, wife's and mother's tears.
　Weep not !

WEEP NOT!
    She it not dead, but asleep. Who would not sleep
    Rather than work and weary and waste and weep
    Here in life's fever, faction, fear, and fret?
    Her cheeks and lashes will never more be wet:
    He called her back ere her heart had learned to ache ;
    He loved her much, and took her for her own sake.
Weep not!

After a careful examination of the contents of this volume we do not
hesitate to award to Mr Sladen the title of an Australian poet. That he
may justify our conclusion in more ambitious, more definitely Australian
work is our sincere hope. He has evidently the requisite capacity.

A POETRY OF EXILES.

London : GRIFFITH & FARRAN, St Paul's Churchyard, E.C.

C. E. FULLER & Co., Sydney, N.S.W.

*Published almost simultaneously, and therefore only one critique has
come to hand in time for Publication.*

From the FEDERAL AUSTRALIAN, *Melbourne, May* 31st, 1884.

Many of the Short Pieces are very complete, and indicate what Mr
Sladen is capable of achieving. We are greatly pleased with such little
poems as the " Plaint of the Prodigal Son," "Winter," and "The Poet's
Message." From the last named we give one verse :—

   " God had been good to him, and he endeavoured
     To render God due thankfulness and meed,
   By putting down the obstacles that severed
     Man from his fellow-man, in fact or creed ;
   By singing of the goodness and the gladness
     Of all creation, till impaired by man,
   And pointing out the soothing side of sadness,
     The harmony of the Creator's Plan."

A CATALOGUE OF

NEW AND STANDARD BOOKS

IN GENERAL LITERATURE,

DEVOTIONAL AND RELIGIOUS BOOKS,

AND

Educational Books & Appliances.

Goldsmith introduced to Newbery by Dr. Johnson.

PUBLISHED BY

GRIFFITH & FARRAN,

WEST CORNER OF ST. PAUL'S CHURCHYARD, LONDON.

E. P. DUTTON & Co., NEW YORK.

10M. 3/84.

B

CONTENTS.

WORKS OF TRAVEL.

Important and Interesting Book of Travels.

Unexplored Baluchistan : a Survey, with Observations Astronomical, Geographical, Botanical, &c., of a Route through **Western Baluchistan, Mekran, Bashakird, Persia, Kurdistan,** and **Turkey.** By E. A. FLOYER, F.R.G.S., F.L.S., &c. With Twelve Illustrations and a Map. Price 28s.

Important Work on South Africa.

Eight Months in an Ox-Waggon. Reminiscences of Boer Life. By E. F. SANDEMAN. Demy 8vo., with a Map, cloth, 15s.

A Visit to the United States.

The Other Side : How it Struck Us. Being Sketches of a Winter Visit to the United States and Canada. By C. B. BERRY. Cloth, price 9s.

Our Sketching Tour. By Two of the Artists. With one hundred and seven illustrations, cr. 4to., price 7s. 6d.

Rambles in the Green Lanes of Hampshire, Surrey, Sussex. By the Rev. G. N. GOODWIN, Chaplain to the Forces. I vol., demy 8vo., price 5s.

Adventures in many Lands.

Travel, War, and Shipwreck. By Colonel W. PARKER GILMORE (" Ubique,") author of "The Great Thirst Land," &c. Crown 8vo. Price 3s. 6d.

General Gordon in China: The Story of the " Ever Victorious Army." By S. MOSSMAN. Crown 8vo., cloth elegant, price 3s. 6d.

Travels in Palestine.

" His Native Land." By the Rev. A. J. BINNIE, M.A., Curate of Kenilworth, late Vicar of St. Silas, Leeds. With Preface by the Rev. JOHN MILES MOSS, of Liverpool. With a Photograph of Jerusalem, and a Map of Palestine. Cr. 8vo., cloth, 2s. 6d.

HISTORY & BIOGRAPHY.

Second Edition—revised.

Memories of Seventy Years. By one of a literary family. Edited by Mrs. HERBERT MARTIN. One vol., Crown 8vo., cloth, price 7s. 6d.

A Bookseller of the Last Century. Being some account of the Life of JOHN NEWBERY, and of the Books he published; with a Chapter on the later Newberys. By CHARLES WELSH. [In preparation.

Studies in History, Legend, and Literature. By H. SCHUTZ-WILSON, Author of "Studies and Romances," &c. One vol. Crown 8vo., cloth, bevelled boards, price 7s. 6d.

Records of York Castle, Fortress, Court House, and Prison. By Captain A. W. TWYFORD (the late Governor) and Major ARTHUR GRIFFITHS. Crown 8vo. With Engravings and Photographs. 7s. 6d.

York and York Castle: An Appendix to the "Records of York Castle." By Captain A. W. TWYFORD, F.R.G.S. Cloth, price 10s. 6d.

Historical Sketches of the Reformation. By the Rev. FREDERICK GEORGE LEE, D.C.L., Vicar of All Saints, Lambeth, &c., &c. Post 8vo., price 10s. 6d.

The Crimean Campaign with the Connaught Rangers, 1854—55—56. By Lieut.-Colonel NATHANIEL STEEVENS, late 88th (Connaught Rangers). Demy 8vo., with Map, cloth, 15s.

Memorable Battles in English History; Where Fought, Why Fought, and their Results; with the Military Lives of the Commanders. By W. H. DAVENPORT ADAMS. New and thoroughly Revised Edition, with Frontispiece and Plans of Battles. Two Volumes, crown 8vo., cloth, price 16s.

Ocean and Her Rulers; A Narrative of the Nations who have from the Earliest Ages held Dominion over the Sea, comprising a brief History of Navigation from the Remotest Periods up to the Present Time. By ALFRED ELWES. With 16 Illustrations by WALTER W. MAY. Crown 8vo., cloth, 9s.

HISTORY & BIOGRAPHY—*(continued)*.

The Modern British Plutarch ; or, Lives of Men
Distinguished in the recent History of our Country for their Talents, Virtues, and Achievements. By W. C. TAYLOR, LL.D. 12mo. 4s. 6d., or gilt edges, 5s.

A Life of the Prince Imperial of France.
By ELLEN BARLEE. Demy 8vo., with a Photograph of the Prince. Cloth, price 12s. 6d.

Heroes of History and Legend. Translated by
JOHN LANCELOT SHADWELL from the German "Character-bilder aus Geschichte und Sage," by A. W. GRÜBE. One vol. Crown 8vo., price 3s. 6d.

Pictures of the Past : Memories of Men I have
Met, and Sights I have Seen. By FRANCIS H. GRUNDY, C.E. Crown 8vo., cloth, price 12s.

Six Life Studies of Famous Women. By
M. BETHAM-EDWARDS, Author of "Kitty," "Dr. Jacob," "A Year in Western France," &c. With Six Portraits engraved on Steel. Cloth, price 7s. 6d.

Joan of Arc and the Times of Charles the
Seventh. By Mrs. BRAY. 7s. 6d.

" Readers will rise from its perusal not only with increased information, but with sympathies awakened and elevated."—TIMES.

The Good St. Louis and His Times. By the
same Author. With Portrait. 7s. 6d.

"A valuable and interesting record of Louis' reign."—SPECTATOR.

Tales of the White Cockade. By BARBARA
HUTTON. Illustrated by J. LAWSON. Crown 8vo., cloth, 3s. 6d.

The Fiery Cross, or the Vow of Montrose.
By BARBARA HUTTON. Illustrated by J. LAWSON. Crown 8vo., cloth, 3s. 6d.

Afghanistan : A Short Account of Afghanistan, its
history and our dealings with it. By P. F. WALKER, Barrister-at-Law (late 75th Regiment). Cloth, 2s. 6d.

STANESBY'S ILLUMINATED GIFT BOOKS.

Every page richly printed in Gold and Colours.

The Bridal Souvenir. With a Portrait of the
Princess Royal. Elegantly bound in white morocco, 21*s.*

The Birthday Souvenir. A Book of Thoughts
on Life and Immortality. 12*s. 6d.* cloth ; 18*s.* morocco.

Light for the Path of Life ; from the Holy Scrip-
tures. 12*s.* cloth; 15*s.* calf, gilt edges ; 18*s.* mor. antique.

The Wisdom of Solomon ; from the Book of
Proverbs. 14*s.*, cloth elegant ; 18*s.* calf ; 21*s.* mor. antique.

The Floral Gift. 14s. cloth elegant; 21s. morocco
extra.

Shakespeare's Household Words. With a
Photograph from the Monument at Stratford-on-Avon. New
and Cheaper Edition, 6*s.* cloth elegant ; 10*s. 6d.* mor. antique.

Aphorisms of the Wise and Good. With a
Portrait of Milton. 6*s.* cloth elegant ; 10*s. 6d.* mor. antique.

SCIENCE, USEFUL KNOWLEDGE, & ENTERTAINING ANECDOTE.

The Commercial Products of the Sea ; or,
Marine Contributions to Industry and Art. By P.L.SIMMONDS,
Author of "The Commercial Products of the Vegetable
Kingdom." With numerous Illustrations. New and Cheaper
Edition, price 7*s. 6d.*

Folk-Lore of Shakespeare. By the Rev. J. F.
THISELTON DYER. Demy 8vo., cloth, bevelled boards,
price 14*s.*

Choice Extracts from the Standard Authors.
By the Editor of " Poetry for the Young." In three volumes.
Foolscap 8vo., cloth, elegant, price 2*s. 6d.* each.

USEFUL KNOWLEDGE & ENTERTAINING ANECDOTE—*(continued).*

Snakes. Curiosities and Wonders of Serpent Life.
By Miss CATHERINE C. HOPLEY, Author of "Aunt Jenny's American Pets." Illustrated by A. T. ELWES. Demy 8vo., price 16s.

Talks about Science. By the late THOMAS DUN-
MAN, Physiology Lecturer at the Birkbeck Institution and the Working Men's College. With a Biographical Sketch by CHARLES WELSH. Crown 8vo., cloth, bevelled boards, price 3s. 6d.

Talks About Plants; or, Early Lessons in Botany.
By Mrs. LANCASTER, Author of "Wild Flowers Worth Notice," &c. With Six Coloured Plates and Numerous Wood Engravings. Crown 8vo., cloth, 3s. 6d.

The Four Seasons; A Short Account of the
Structure of Plants, being Four Lectures written for the Working Men's Institute, Paris. With Illustrations. Imperial 16mo., 3s. 6d.

Trees, Plants, and Flowers, their Beauties,
Uses, and Influences. By Mrs. R. LEE. With Coloured Groups of Flowers from Drawings by JAMES ANDREWS. Second Thousand. 8vo., cloth, gilt edges, 10s. 6d.

Everyday Things; or, Useful Knowledge respecting
the principal Animal, Vegetable, and Mineral Substances in Common Use. 18mo., cloth 1s. 6d.

Infant Amusements; or, How to Make a Nursery
Happy. With practical Hints to Parents and Nurses on the Moral and Physical Training of Children. By W. H. G. KINGSTON. Cloth, 3s. 6d.

Female Christian Names, and their Teachings.
By MARY E. BROMFIELD. Beautifully printed on Toned Paper. Imp. 32mo., Cloth, gilt edges, 1s. French Morocco, 2s. Calf or Morocco, 4s.

Our Sailors; or, Anecdotes of the Engagements and
Gallant Deeds of the British Navy. By the late W. H. G. KINGSTON. Revised and brought down to date by G. A. HENTY. With Frontispiece. Crown 8vo., cloth elegant, 3s. 6d.

USEFUL KNOWLEDGE & ENTERTAINING ANECDOTE—*(continued)*.

Our Soldiers ; or, Anecdotes of the Campaigns and
Gallant Deeds of the British Army during the Reign of Her
Majesty Queen Victoria. By the late W. H. G. KINGSTON.
Revised and brought down to date by G. A. HENTY. With
Frontispiece. Crown 8vo., cloth elegant, 3*s.* 6*d.*

Anecdotes of the Habits and Instincts of
Animals. By Mrs. R. LEE. Illustrated by HARRISON WEIR.
Post 8vo., Cloth, 3*s.* 6*d.*

Anecdotes of the Habits and Instincts of
Birds, Reptiles, and Fishes. By Mrs. R. LEE. Illustrated by
HARRISON WEIR. Post 8vo., Cloth, 3*s.* 6*d.*

Ancestral Stories and Traditions of Great
Families. Illustrative of English History. With Frontispiece.
By the late JOHN TIMBS, F.S.A. Cloth, 7*s.* 6*d.*

HANDBOOKS FOR THE HOUSEHOLD.

Ambulance Lectures : or, What to do in Cases of
Accidents or Sudden Illness. By L. A. WEATHERLEY,
M.D., Lecturer to the Ambulance Department, Order of St.
John of Jerusalem in England. With numerous Illustrations.
Cloth, thoroughly revised, price 1*s.*

Lectures on Domestic Hygiene and Home
Nursing. By L. A. WEATHERLEY, M.D., Member of
the Royal College of Surgeons of England ; Fellow of the
Obstetrical Society of London, &c. Illustrated. Cloth, limp, 1*s.*

The Young Wife's Own Book. A Manual of
Personal and Family Hygiene, containing everything that the
young wife and mother ought to know concerning her own
health at the most important periods of her life, and that of
her children. By L. A. WEATHERLEY, M.D., Author of
"Ambulance Lectures," "Hygiene and Home Nursing," &c.
Fcap. 8vo., stiff boards, price 1*s.*

HANDBOOKS FOR THE HOUSEHOLD—*(continued)*.

The Food we Eat, and why we Eat it, and
whence its Comes. By Dr. J. MILNER FOTHERGILL. Edited by A. MILNER FOTHERGILL. Fcap. 8vo., cloth, limp, price 1s.

The Care and Treatment of the Insane in
Private Dwellings. By L. A. WEATHERLEY, M.D., C.M., Member of the Royal College of Surgeons of England, Member of the Medico-Psychological Associations of Great Britain, Fellow of the Obstetric Society of London. Fcap. 8vo., cloth, price 1s. 6d.

Popular Lectures on Plain and High-class
Cookery. By a former Staff Teacher of the National Training School of Cookery. Cloth, 1s. 6d.

The Art of Washing; Clothes, Personal, and
House. By Mrs. A. A. STRANGE BUTSON. Cloth, price 1s. 6d.

Artizan Cookery, and how to Teach it. By
a Pupil of the National Training School for Cookery, South Kensington. Sewed, 6d.

The Stage in the Drawing Room; or the
Theatre at Home. Practical Hints on Amateur Acting for Amateur Actors. By HENRY J. DAKIN. Fully illustrated, price One Shilling. Uniform with the "Household Handbooks."

FICTION, &c.

A New Book of American Humour and Pathos.

Cape Cod Folks. By SALLY PRATT M'LEAN.
Crown 8vo., cloth, elegant bevelled boards, price 5s.

"We have seen few stories that opened so many unusual views of mankind as 'Cape Cod Folks.' . . . For those who seek amusement there is something to make the reader chuckle on every page."—*Athenæum.*

"An excellent story.' —*Morning Post.*

Percy Pomo; or, The Autobiography of a South Sea
Islander. A Tale of Life and Adventure (Missionary, Trading, and Slaving) in the South Pacific. Crown 8vo., cloth, price 6s.

Halek; an Autobiographical Fragment. By JOHN H.
NICHOLSON. Crown 8vo., price 7s. 6d.

FICTION, &c.—*(continued)*.

Hillsland as it was Seventy Years ago. A
Story in One Volume. By the Rev. F. H. MORGAN. Crown
8vo., cloth, price 5*s.*

Lois Leggatt ; a Memoir. By FRANCIS CARR,
Author of "Left Alone," "Tried by Fire," &c. One vol.,
crown 8vo., price 6*s.*, cloth.

Worthless Laurels. A Story of the Stage. By
EMILY CARRINGTON. Three vols., crown 8vo., 31*s.* 6*d.*

Louis : or, Doomed to the Cloister. A Tale of
Religious Life in the time of Louis XIV. Founded on Fact.
By M. J. HOPE. Dedicated by permission to Dean Stanley.
Three vols., crown 8vo., 31*s.* 6*d.*

Tried by Fire. By FRANCIS CARR, Author of "Left
Alone," &c. Three vols., crown 8vo., 31*s.* 6*d.*

A Journey to the Centre of the Earth.
From the French of JULES VERNE. With 52 Illustrations by
RIOU. New Edition. Post 8vo., 6*s.* ; or bevelled boards,
gilt edges, 7*s.* 6*d.*

The Secret of the Sands ; or, The Water Lily and
her Crew. By HARRY COLLINGWOOD. Two vols., crown
8vo., cloth, gilt tops, 12*s.*

Elsie Grey ; A Tale of Truth. By CECIL CLARKE.
Crown 8vo., cloth, 5*s.*

Sister Clarice ; An Old Maid's Story. By Mrs.
HUNTER HODGSON, "A Soldier's Daughter." Crown 8vo.,
cloth boards, price 3*s.* 6*d.*

St. Nicholas Eve and other Tales. By MARY
C. ROWSELL. Crown 8vo., price 7*s.* 6*d.*

Wothorpe-by-Stamford. A Tale of Bygone Days.
By C. HOLDICH. Five Engravings. Cloth, 3*s.* 6*d.*

POETRY AND BELLES-LETTRES.

A Bird's-Eye View of English Literature:
From the Seventh Century to the Present Time. By HENRY GREY, Author of "The Classics for the Million," "A Key to the Waverley Novels," &c., &c. Fcap. 8vo., limp cloth, price 1s.
"Very clear and accurate."—*Schoolmaster.* "A dainty little volume."—*Life.*

New and cheaper edition price 1s.; or cloth, price 2s.
The Classics for the Million; being an Epitome
in English of the Works of the Principal Greek and Latin Authors. By the same author.
"An admirable resumé."—*John Bull.*
"A most useful work."—*Edinburgh Courant.*

Music in Song: From Chaucer to Tennyson. Being
a Selection of Extracts, descriptive of the power, influence, and effects of music. Compiled by L. L. CARMELA KOELLE, with an introduction by Dr. JOHN STAINER. Printed in red and black on Dutch hand-made paper, and bound in parchment. Price 3s. 6d.

The Raven. By EDGAR ALLAN POE. A sumptuously
illustrated edition in elegant cloth boards, gilt edges, price 3s. 6d.; or in a chromo cover, with fringed edge, price 6s.

The Evening Hymn. By the Rev. JOHN KEBLE.
A sumptuously illustrated edition, uniform with the above, price 3s. 6d.; or in a chromo cover, with fringed edge, price 6s.

Rhymes in Council: Aphorisms Versified—185.
By S. C. HALL, F.S.A. Dedicated by permission to the Grandchildren of the Queen. 4to., printed in black with red borders. Cloth elegant, 2s. 6d.

Masterpieces of Antique Art. From the cele-
brated collections in the Vatican, the Louvre, and the British Museum. By STEPHEN THOMPSON, Author of "Old English Homes." Twenty-five Examples in Permanent Photography. Super-Royal Quarto. Elegantly bound, cloth gilt, Two Guineas.

POETRY AND BELLES-LETTRES—(*continued*).

The Seasons; a Poem by the Rev. O. RAYMOND, LL.B., Author of "Paradise," and other Poems. Fcap. 8vo., with Four Illustrations. Cloth, 2*s.* 6*d.*

The Golden Queen: a Tale of Love, War, and Magic. By EDWARD A. SLOANE. Cloth, gilt edges, 6*s.*; or plain edges, 5*s.*

Grandma's Attic Treasures; A Story of Old Time Memories. By MARY D. BRINE. Illustrated with numerous Wood Engravings, executed in the best style of the art. Suitable for a Christmas Present. Small quarto, cloth, gilt edges, price 9*s.*

A Woodland Idyll. By Miss PHŒBE ALLEN. It is dedicated to Principal Shairp, and is an attempt to represent allegorically the relative positions of Nature, Art, and Science in our World. Cloth, 2*s.* 6*d.*

Stories from Early English Literature, with some Account of the Origin of Fairy Tales, Legends and Traditionary Lore. Adapted to the use of Young Students. By Miss S. J. VENABLES DODDS. Crown 8vo., price 5*s.*

Similitudes. Like likes Like. 16mo., cloth, bevelled boards, price 2*s.* 6*d.*

A Key to all the Waverley Novels in Chronological Sequence. By HENRY GREY, Author of "Classics for the Million." Price Threepence.

BIRTHDAY AND ANNIVERSARY BOOKS.

The Churchman's Daily Remembrancer, with Poetical Selections for the Christian Year, with the Kalendar and Table of Lessons of the English Church, for the use of both Clergy and Laity.

	s.	d.			s.	d.
Cloth extra, red edges	2	0	Morocco, bevelled ...	...	5	0
French Morocco, limp	3	0	Morocco bevelled, clasp	...	6	0
French Morocco, circuit or tuck	3	6	Russia, limp	...	6	0
Persian Morocco, limp	3	6	Levant Morocco, limp ...	...	6	6
Persian Morocco, circuit ...	4	6	Russia, circuit	...	7	6
Calf or Morocco, limp	4	6	Russia limp, in drop case	...	9	0

With Twelve Photographs, 2s. extra.

BIRTHDAY AND ANNIVERSARY BOOKS—*(continued)*.

The Book of Remembrance for every Day

in the Year. Containing Choice Extracts from the best Authors, and the exact place indicated whence the Quotation is taken, with Blank Spaces for recording Birthdays, Marriages, and other Anniversaries. Beautifully printed in red and black. Imperial 32mo.

"A charming little memorial of love and friendship, and happily executed as conceived. For a birthday or other Anniversary nothing can be prettier or more appropriate." —BOOKSELLER. *" Beautifully got up."* —LEEDS MERCURY.

May be had in the following Styles of Binding :—

	s. d.		s. d.
Cloth extra, plain edges ...	2 0	Calf or Morocco, limp, red under gold edges	5 0
Cloth Elegant, bevelled boards, gilt edges	2 6	Morocco, bevelled boards, do...	7 6
French Morocco, limp, gilt edges	3 0	Ditto, with gilt clasp	8 6
Persian Morocco, bevelled boards, red under gold edges	4 0	Russia. limp, elegant, with gilt clasp	10 0
Persian Morocco, with clasp ...	4 6		

With Twelve Beautiful Photographs.

	s. d.		s. d.
Cloth elegant	5 0	Morocco, bevelled	12 6
French Morocco, limp, gilt edges	8 6	Russia, limp, extra ...	15 0
Calf or morocco, limp	10 0	Levant Morocco, elegant ...	18 0

Anniversary Text Book ; a Book of Scripture

Verse and Sacred Song for Every Day in the Year. Interleaved.

May be had in the following Styles of Binding:—

	s. d.		s. d.
Cloth, bevelled boards, white edges	1 0	Imitation Ivory, rims	3 0
		Morocco, elegant, rims	4 6
Cloth, gilt boards, gilt edges ...	1 6	Morocco, bevelled, and clasp ...	4 6
,, ,, ,, rims	2 0	Russia, limp, red under gold edges	4 6
French Morocco, limp	2 0		
Calf or Morocco ,, ...	2 6	Ivory, rims	7 6

DEVOTIONAL AND RELIGIOUS BOOKS.

A Catechism of Church Doctrine. For Younger

Children. By the Rev. T. S. HALL, M.A., The Vicarage, Hythe. Price 1*d.*, paper; 2*d.*, cloth.

Sermons for Children. By A. DECOPPET, Pastor

of the Reformed Church in Paris. Translated from the French by MARIE TAYLOR. With an Introduction by Mrs. HENRY REEVE. Price 3*s.* 6*d.*

The Churchman's Altar Manual and Guide

to Holy Communion, together with the Collects, Epistles, an Gospels, and a Selection of appropriate Hymns. Borders un Rubrics in red.

Three Editions of this Manual are now issued. The following are the sizes and prices :—Royal 32mo., with Rubrics and Borders in red, cloth, 2*s.*, or with Eight Photos., 4*s.* (A Confirmation Card is presented with this edition.) Large Type Edition, cloth, red edges, 2*s.* Cheap Edition, for distribution, cloth flush, 6*d.* ; or red edges, 9*d.*

For the Use of Newly-Confirmed and others.

The Young Communicant's Manual. Con-

taining Instructions and Preparatory Prayers in accordance with the Church's directions for Preparations; Form of Self-Examination; the Services for the Holy Communion, with appropriate Devotions, Intercessions, and Thanksgivings; Hymns, &c. Price 1*s.*

Cheap Edition for distribution, cloth flush, price 6*d.*, or cloth boards, red edges, 9*d.*

Bishop Ken's Approach to the Holy Altar.

With an Address to Young Communicants. New and Cheaper Edition.

	s. d.				s. d.
Limp cloth	0 8	Calf or morocco, limp ...	...	3 6
Superior cloth, red edges ...	1 0	Morocco, bevelled ...	...	4 6
French morocco, limp	1 6	Russia, limp	...	4 6

With Photographs, 2s. extra.

*** Clergymen wishing to introduce this Manual can have Specimen Copy, with prices for quantities, post free for six stamps on application.

A Lent Manual for Busy People and for the

Young. 32mo. sewed, 3d., or bound in cloth with red edges, price 6d.

The Song of Solomon, rendered in English Verse,

in accordance with the most approved translation from the Hebrew and Septuagint. By the Rev. JAMES PRATT, D.D. With 7 Illustrations. Crown 8vo., cloth, 3*s.* 6*d.*

An Epitome of Anglican Church History

from the Earliest Ages to the Present Time. Compiled from various sources by ELLEN WEBLEY-PARRY. Demy 8vo., cloth boards, 5*s.*

DEVOTIONAL AND RELIGIOUS BOOKS—(*continued*).

The Life Militant. Plain Sermons for Cottage
Homes. By ELLELL. Crown 8vo., price 6*s.*

The Way of Prayer; a Book of Devotions, for
use in Church and at Home. Compiled by Rev. H. W. MILLAR
M.A. Cloth, red edges, 1*s.*

Bogatsky's Golden Treasury for the Children of
God, consisting of devotional and practical observations for
every day in the year. Fcap. 16mo, with purple border lines,
price One Shilling.

Also kept in various leather bindings.
A new and elegantly-printed edition of this well-known work.

Foreign Churches in relating to the Anglican; an
Essay towards Re-Union. By W. J. E. BENNETT, M.A.,
Priest of the English Church, Vicar of Frome, Selwood,
Somerset. Demy 8vo., price 5*s.*

The Churchman's Manual of Family and Private
Devotion, compiled from the writings of English Divines, with
Graces and Devotions for the Seasons, Litanies, and an entirely
new selection of Hymns. Super royal 32mo., price 1*s.* 6*d.*

ALSO KEPT IN VARIOUS LEATHER BINDINGS.
MINIATURE SERIES OF DEVOTIONAL BOOKS. Small square
32mo, 6*d.* each.

Whispers of Love and Wisdom. By ANNIE
CAZENOVE.

Fragments in Prose and Verse. By ANNIE
CAZENOVE.

Cut Diamonds. By ELLEN GUBBINS.
These three books may be had in a cloth case, price 2*s.*; or
leather, 3*s.* 6*d.* They may all be had in various styles of
leather binding.

Traveller's Joy by the Wayside of Life. By
ELLEN GUBBINS, Author of "Cut Diamonds," &c. Square
32mo., uniform with the above series, price 6*d.*

DEVOTIONAL AND RELIGIOUS BOOKS—*(continued).*

The Children's Daily Help for the Christian Year.

Taken from the Psalms and Lessons. Selected by E. G.
Price 1*s.* 6*d.*, or bevelled boards, gilt edges, 2*s.*
Also kept in various leather bindings.

Now publishing in Monthly Parts, price One Shilling each.

Sermons for the Church's Year.   Original and

Selected. By the Rev. W. BENHAM, B.D., Rector of St.
Edmund the King, London, and one of the six preachers in
Canterbury Cathedral. Sixty-four pages, demy 8vo.

"We hope that Mr. Benham's very useful venture will prove successful, as it
well deserves to be."—*Church Union Gazette.*

"We cordially appreciate the necessity for a revival of interest in the best
sermons of the past, if only because the perusal of them may tend to elevate the
literary style of modern preachers."—*Church Review.*

Confirmation ; or, Called and Chosen and Faithful.

By the Author of "The Gospel in the Church's Seasons Series."
With Preface by the Very Rev. the DEAN OF CHESTER. Fcap.
8vo., cloth limp, 9*d.* ; cloth boards, red edges, 1*s.*

A Cheaper Edition for Distribution, price 3*d.*

Dr. Lee's Altar Services.   Edited by the Rev.

Dr. F. G. LEE, D.C.L., F.S.A. Containing the complete
Altar Services of the Church, beautifully printed in red and
black at the Chiswick Press, enriched with Ornamental Capitals,
&c., in Three Volumes ; One Volume, folio size, 15 × 10 × 1½
inches ; and two Volumes 4to., containing the Epistles and
Gospels separately, each 12 × 9 × ¾ inches.

The Set, in Turkey Morocco, plain	...	...	£7 7 0
,, Best Levant Morocco, inlaid cross	...	...	£10 10 0

The Folio Volume, which contains all the Services of the Altar,
may be had separately—

Turkey Morocco, plain ...	...	...	...	£3 3 0
Best Levant Morocco, inlaid cross	...	...	...	£4 4 0

** The work can also be bound specially to order in cheaper or
more expensive styles.

Messrs. GRIFFITH & FARRAN have a few copies remaining
of this rare and valuable work, which is not only the best book for
the purpose for which it is designed, but is one of the finest specimens
of typographical art which the Chiswick Press has produced.

DEVOTIONAL AND RELIGIOUS BOOKS—*(continued)*.

The Preacher's Promptuary of Anecdote.
Stories New and Old. Arranged, indexed, and classified by Rev. W. FRANK SHAW, Author of "The Mourner's Manual," "Sermon Sketches," &c. One hundred short and pithy stories, suitable for the pulpit, evening classes, &c., each pointing a moral or illustrating some doctrine. Cloth boards, price

Lazarus. By the Very Rev. The DEAN OF WELLS.
New Edition.

The Churchman's Text Book. For every day in
the Christian Year. Containing a Poetical Extract and an appropriate Text, with the Holy days of the Church duly recorded. An elegantly printed and daintily bound little volume in diamond 48mo. 3¾ by 2¼ inches, cloth, limp, red edges, 6*d*. It may also be had in various leather bindings and interleaved with ruled Writing Paper, 6*d*. extra.

The Seven Words from the Cross. Printed
in red and black upon best hand-made paper, and bound in parchment covers, uniform with "Music in Song." Price 3*s*. 6*d*.

On the Wings of a Dove; or, the Life of a Soul:
An Allegory. Illustrated by SISTER E.—C. S. J. B. CLEWER. Demy 16mo., with eight Illustrations. Cloth 1*s*. 6*d*.

Emblems of Christian Life. Illustrated by
W. HARRY ROGERS, in One Hundred Original Designs, from the Writings of the Fathers, Old English Poets, &c. Printed by WHITTINGHAM, with borders and Initials in red. Square 8vo., price 10*s*. 6*d*. cloth elegant, gilt edges; 21*s*. Turkey morocco antique.

A New Inexpensive Confirmation Card.
Printed in red and black, size 5 × 3½ inches. Sold in Packets of Twelve Cards for 6*d*.

An Illuminated Certificate of Confirmation
and First Communion. Printed in gold and colours, size 6 × 4½ inches. Price 2*d*.

An "In Memoriam" Card. Beautifully printed
in silver or gold, price 2*d*.
₊ *A reduction made on taking a quantity of the above Cards.*

AMERICAN SERMONS
AND
THEOLOGICAL BOOKS.
.PUBLISHED BY

E. P. DUTTON and CO., *New York, U.S.A.,*
AND SOLD IN ENGLAND BY
GRIFFITH AND FARRAN.

Brooks, the Rev. Phillips, D.D., Rector of
Trinity Church, Boston.

Influence of Jesus. Being the Bohlen Lecture for 1879. Eighth Thousand. Crown 8vo., cloth, price 3s. 6d.

Sermons. Thirteenth Thousand. Crown 8vo., cloth, price 5s.

Chapman, Rev. Dr.

Sermons upon the Ministry, Worship, and Doctrine of the Church. New Edition. Crown 8vo., price 5s.

Clergyman's Visiting List, in morocco, with tuck for the pocket. Foolscap, price 7s. 6d.

Doane, Rt. Rev. Wm. Croswell, D.D.,
Bishop of Albany.

Mosaics; or, the Harmony of Collect, Epistle, and Gospel for the Sundays of the Christian Year. Cr. 8vo., cloth, 6s.

Hallam, Rev. Robert A., D.D.

Lectures on the Morning Prayer. 12mo., 5s.

Lectures on Moses. 12mo., cloth, 3s. 6d.

Handbook of Church Terms.

A Pocket Dictionary; or, Brief Explanation of Words in Common Use relating to the Order, Worship, Architecture, Vestments, Usages, and Symbolism of the Church, as employed in Christian Art. Paper, 9d.; cloth, 1s. 6d.

Hobart, Rev. John Henry, D.D., formerly
Bishop of New York.

Festivals and Fasts. A Companion for the Festivals and Fasts of the Protestant Episcopal Church, principally selected and altered from Nelson's Companion. With Forms of Devotion. Twenty-third Edition. 12mo., 5s.

Hodges, Rev. Wm., D.D.

Baptism : Tested by Scripture and History; or, the Teaching of the Holy Scriptures, and the Practice and Teaching of the Christian Church in every age succeeding the Apostolic, compared in relation to the Subjects and Modes of Baptism. 6s.

Huntington, Rt. Rev. F. D., Bishop of
Central New York.

Christian Believing and Living. Sermons. Fifth Edition. 12mo., 3s. 6d.

Helps to a Holy Lent. 208 pages, crown 8vo., 2s. 6d.

Sermons for the People. Crown 8vo., cloth, 3s. 6d.

Odenheimer, the Rt. Rev. Wm. H., D.D.,
late Bishop of New Jersey.

Sermons, with Portrait and Memoir. Edited by his Wife. Crown 8vo., 5s.

Staunton, Rev. William, D.D.

Ecclesiastical Dictionary, containing Definitions of Terms, and Explanations and Illustrations of Subjects pertaining to the History, Ritual, Discipline, Worship, Ceremonies, and Usages of the Christian Church. 8vo. 746 pp., 7s. 6d.

Vinton, Rev. Alexander H.

Sermons. Fourth Edition. 330 pages, 3s. 6d.

Vinton, Francis, S.T.D., D.C.L.

Manual Commentary on the General Canon Law of the Protestant Episcopal Church. 8vo., cloth, 5s.

Williams, Right Rev. John, D.D., Bishop
of Connecticut.

Studies on the English Reformation. 12mo., cloth, 3s. 6d.

Wilson, Rev. Wm. D., D.D.

The Church Identified. By a reference to the History of its Origin, Extension, and Perpetuation, with Special Reference to the Protestant Episcopal Church in the United States. Revised Edition, 12mo., 439 pp. 6s.

EDUCATIONAL WORKS.

GOOD HANDWRITING.

GEORGE DARNELL's COPY-BOOKS,

After over a quarter of a century of public favour, are every-where acknowledged as the best for simplicity and thoroughness. With these Copy-Books the pupil advances in the art of writing with ease and rapidity, while the labour of the teacher is very greatly lightened. They are used in nearly all the best schools in Great Britain and the Colonies, and are adapted to the New Educational Code.

ADVANTAGES OF THE SYSTEM.

I. It is the production of an experienced Schoolmaster.
II. It gradually advances from the Simple Stroke to a superior Small Hand.
III. The assistance given in the Primal lesson is reduced as the learner progresses, until all guidance is safely withdrawn.
IV. The number and variety of the copies secure attention, and prevent the pupils copying their own writing, as in books with single head-lines.
V. The system insures the progress of the learner, and greatly lightens the labours of the teacher.

Darnell's Universal Twopenny Copy-Books,

for the Standards. 16 Nos., Fcap. 4to. Being a series of sixteen copy-books, by GEORGE DARNELL, the first ten of which have on every alternate line appropriate and carefully written copies in Pencil coloured Ink, to be first written over and then imitated, the remaining numbers having Black Head-lines for imitation only, THE WHOLE GRADUALLY ADVANCING FROM A SIMPLE STROKE TO A SUPERIOR SMALL HAND.

STANDARD I.
1. Elementary.
2. Single and Double Letters.
3. Large Text (Short Words).

STANDARD II.
3. Large Text (Short Words).
4. Large Text (Short Words).
5. Text, Large Text, and Figures.

STANDARD III.
6. Text, Round, Capitals & Figures.
7. Text, Round and Small.
8. Text, Round, Small & Figures.

STANDARD IV.
9. Text, Round, Small & Figures.
10. Text, Round, Small & Figures.
11. Round, Small and Figures.

STANDARD V.
12. Round, Small and Figures.
13. Round and Small.
14. Round and Small.

STANDARD VI.
15. Small Hand.
16. Small Hand.

CopY-Books—(*continued*).

Darnell's Large Post Copy-Books. A Sure
and Certain Road to a Good Handwriting. 16 Nos., 6*d.* each.

Darnell's Foolscap Copy-Books. A Sure Guide
to a Good Handwriting, on the same plan. 24 Nos., 3*d.* each,
green covers; or on a superior paper, marble covers, 4*d.* each.

HISTORY.

Britannia; a Collection of the Principal Passages in
Latin Authors that refer to this Island, with Vocabulary and
Notes. By T. S. CAYZER. Illustrated with a Map and 29
Woodcuts. Crown 8vo., cloth, 3*s.* 6*d.*

True Stories from Ancient History, chrono-
logically arranged from the Creation of the World to the Death
of Charlemagne. Twelfth Edition. 12mo., 5*s.* cloth.

Mrs. Trimmer's Concise History of England,
Revised and brought down to the Present Time. By Mrs.
MILNER. With Portraits of the Sovereigns. 5*s.* cloth

Historical Reading Books. By OSCAR BROWNING,
M.A., King's College, Cambridge. Fully illustrated. They
consist of four volumes of about 150 or 200 pages each. The
object is to give a knowledge of general English History. The
First Reader contains easy episodes from the whole course of
English History, arranged in chronological order. The Second
Reader consists of less easy episodes, arranged on the same
plan. The Third and Fourth Readers contain a short History
of England, divided into two parts. By this means the instruction is given in successive layers, as it were, and the
inconvenience of confining the lowest Standards to the earlier
part of English History is avoided. The Readers are copiously
illustrated, and printed in conspicuous type.

Book	I.	...	about	150	pages	...	price	1/-
,,	II.	...	,,	180	,,	...	,,	1/3
,,	III.	...	,,	200	,,	...	,,	1/6
,,	IV.	...	,,	250	,,	...	,,	1/6

GRIFFITH & FARRAN'S
NEW GEOGRAPHICAL READERS.

To meet the requirements of Circular 228.

By J. R. BLAKISTON, M.A.,

Trinity College, Cambridge, Author of " The Teacher."

BOOK I., FOR STANDARD I.

With a Map and many Illustrations. Fcap. 8vo., cloth limp, 8*d.*, boards, 10*d.*

BOOK II., FOR STANDARD II.

With a Map of England and numerous Illustrations. Fcap. 8vo., cloth boards, price 1*s.*

BOOK III., FOR STANDARD III.

With 13 Maps and 18 Illustrations. Fcap. 8vo., cloth boards, price 1*s.* 3*d.*

The other Volumes will be Ready Shortly.

Each Volume contains the right number of chapters and of pages to satisfy all the requirements of the Code and the recent Circular.

*** Specimen copies post free on receipt of half the published price.

GEOGRAPHY.

Pictorial Geography, for the Instruction of Children. Illustrates at a glance the Various Geographical Terms in such a manner as to at once impart clear and definite ideas respecting them. On a Sheet 30 by 22 inches, printed in colours, 1s. 6d. ; Mounted on Rollers and Varnished, 3s. 6d.

"Forms an excellent introduction to the study of maps."—SCHOOL BOARD CHRONICLE.

Gaultier's Familiar Geography. With a concise Treatise on the Artificial Sphere, and Two Coloured Maps, illustrative of the principal Geographical Terms. Cloth, 3s.

Butler's Outline Maps, and Key, or Geo-graphical and Biographical Exercises : with a Set of Coloured Outline Maps, designed for the Use of Young Persons. By the late WILLIAM BUTLER. Enlarged by the Author's Son, J. O. BUTLER. Price 4s.

GRAMMAR, &c.

A Compendious Grammar, and Philological Handbook of the English Language, for the Use of Schools and Candidates for the Army and Civil Service Examinations. By J. G. COLQUHOUN, Esq., Barrister-at-Law. Cloth, 2s. 6d.

Darnell, G. Grammar made Intelligible to Children. Being a Series of short and simple Rules, with ample Explanations of Every Difficulty, and copious Exercises for Parsing ; in Language adapted to the comprehension of very young Students. New and Revised Edition. Cloth, 1s.

Darnell, G. Introduction to English Gram-mar. Price 3d. Being the first 32 pages of "Grammar made Intelligible."

Darnell, T. Parsing Simplified ; an Intro-duction and Companion to all Grammars ; consisting of Plain and Easy Rules, with Parsing Lessons to each. Cloth, 1s.

In parchment cover, price Sixpence.

Don't : a Manual of Mistakes and Improprieties more or less prevalent in Conduct and Speech. By CENSOR.

GRAMMAR, &c.—*(continued)*.

A Word to the Wise ; or, Hints on the Current
Improprieties of Expression in Writing and Speaking. By
PARRY GWYNNE. Uniform with " Don't," price 1*s.*

The Letter H, Past, Present, and Future.
Rules for the silent H, based on Contemporary Usage, and an
Appeal in behalf of WH. By ALFRED LEACH. Cloth limp.
Price One Shilling.

Harry Hawkins's H-Book ; showing how he
learned to aspirate his H's. Sewed, 6*d.*

Darnell, G. Short and Certain Road to
Reading. Being a Series of EASY LESSONS in which the
Alphabet is so divided as to enable the Child to read many
Pages of Familiar Phrases before he has learned half the letters.
Cloth, 6*d.*; or in 4 parts, paper covers, 1½*d.* each.

Sheet Lessons. Being Extracts from the above,
printed in very large bold type. Price, for the Set of Six
Sheets, 6*d.* ; or, neatly mounted on boards, 3*s.*

Exercises in English. Including Questions in
Analysis, Parsing, Grammar, Spelling, Prefixes, Suffixes,
Word-building, &c. By HENRY ULLYETT, B. Sc., St. Mary's
Sch., Folkestone. These cards are supplied in packets of 30
cards each. Standard VII. has 24. They are provided for
Standards II., III., IV., V., VI., VII., price 1*s.* each. The
whole series is expressly prepared to meet the requirements of
the Murdella Code.

ARITHMETIC, ALGEBRA, & GEOMETRY.

Darnell, G. Arithmetic made Intelligible to
Children. Being a Series of GRADUALLY ADVANCING EXER-
CISES, intended to employ the Reason rather than the Memory
of the Pupil ; with ample Explanations of every Difficulty, in
Language adapted to the comprehension of very young Students.
Cloth, 1*s.* 6*d.*

** This work may be had in Three Parts:—Part I., price 6*d.*
Part II., price 9*d.* Part III., price 6*d.*

A KEY to Parts II. & III., price 1*s.* (Part I. does not require a
Key.)

ARITHMETIC, ALGEBRA, & GEOMETRY—*(continued)*.

Cayzer, T. S. One Thousand Arithmetical
TESTS, or THE EXAMINER'S ASSISTANT. Specially adapted, by a novel arrangement of the subject, for Examination Purposes, but also suited for general use in Schools. With a complete set of Examples and Models of Work. Cloth, 1*s*. 6*d*.
All the operations of Arithmetic are presented under Forty Heads, and on opening at any one of the Examination Papers, a complete set of examples appears, carefully graduated.

Key with Solutions of all the Examples in
the One Thousand Arithmetical Tests. Price 4*s*. 6*d*. cloth.
THE ANSWERS only, price 1*s*. 6*d*. cloth.

One Thousand Algebraical Tests ; on the same
plan. 8vo. Cloth 2*s*. 6*d*.
ANSWERS TO THE ALGEBRAICAL TESTS, 2*s*. 6*d*. cloth.

Theory and Practice of the Metric System of
Weights and Measures. By Professor LEONE LEVI, F.S.A., F.S.S. Third Edition. Sewed, 1*s*.

An Aid to Arithmetic. By E. DIVER, M.D. Fcap.
8vo., cloth, price 6*d*.

The Essentials of Geometry, Plane and Solid,
as taught in Germany and France. For Students preparing for Examination, Cadets in Naval and Military Schools, Technical Classes, &c. By J. R. MORELL, formerly one of Her Majesty's Inspectors of Schools. With numerous Diagrams. Cloth, 2*s*.

ELEMENTARY FRENCH & GERMAN WORKS.

L'Abécédaire of French Pronunciation. A
Manual for Teachers and Students. By G. LEPRÉVOST (of Paris), Professor of Languages. Crown 8vo. Cloth, 2*s*.

Le Babillard : an Amusing Introduction to the
French Language. By a FRENCH LADY. Ninth Edition. 16 Plates. Cloth, 2*s*.

FRENCH & GERMAN WORKS—*(continued).*

Les Jeunes Narrateurs, ou Petits Contes
Moraux. With a Key to the Difficult Words and Phrases. Third Edition. 18mo. Cloth, 2s.

The Pictorial French Grammar. For the Use
of Children. Forming a most pleasant and easy introduction to the Language. By MARIN DE LA VOYE. With 80 illustrations. Fcap. 8vo. Cloth, 1s. 6d.

Bellenger's French Word and Phrase Book;
containing a Select Vocabulary and Dialogues. Cloth limp, 1s.

Der Schwätzer; or, The Prattler. An Amusing
Introduction to the German Language. Sixteen Illustrations. Cloth, 2s.

NEW BOOK ON SCIENCE TEACHING.

Adopted by the London School Board.

Preparation for Science Teaching: a Manual of
Suggestions to Teachers. By JOHN SPANTON, Translator of Chevreul's Book on " Colour," &c. Small crown 8vo., price 1s. 6d.

GRIFFITH & FARRAN'S NEEDLEWORK MANUALS AND APPLIANCES.

RECOMMENDED BY THE EDUCATION DEPARTMENT.

The Invariable Stocking Scale will suit any size
or any Wool. Designed by Miss J. HEATH, Senior Examiner of Needlework to the School Board for London. On a wall sheet 30 inches by 22 inches, price 9d. plain, or mounted on roller and varnished, price 2s. 6d. *UNIFORM WITH THE SERIES OF*

NEEDLEWORK, &C.—(*continued*).

Needlework Demonstration Sheets (19 in
number). Exhibiting by Diagrams and Descriptions the
formation of the Stitches in Elementary Needlework. By Mrs.
A. FLOYER. 30 by 22 inches, price 9*d.* each ; or, mounted on
rollers and varnished, 2*s.* 6*d.*

Plain Needlework, arranged in Six Standards, with
Hints for the Management of Class and Appendix on Simul-
taneous Teaching. By Mrs. A. FLOYER. Sewed, 6*d.*

Plain Knitting and Mending, arranged in Six
Standards, with Diagrams. By the same Author. Sewed, 6*d.*

Plain Cutting out for Standards IV., V., and
VI., as now required by the Government Educational Depart-
ment. Adapted to the Principles of Elementary Geometry.
By the same Author. Sewed, 1*s.*

A Set of Diagrams referred to in the Book may be
had separately, printed on stout paper and enclosed in an
envelope. Price 1*s.*

Sectional Paper, for use with the above, 9*d.* per quire.

Lined Paper, for "Extensions." 36in. by 46in.
Price 1*s.* 3*d.* per dozen sheets.

Threaders. 5d. per 100; postage 3d. extra.

Plain Hints for those who have to Examine
Needlework, whether for Government Grants, Prize Associations,
or local Managers ; to which is added Skeleton Demonstration
Lessons to be used with the Demonstration Frames, and a
Glossary of Terms used in the Needlework required from the
Scholars in Public Elementary Schools. By Mrs. A. FLOYER,
Author of "Plain Needlework." Price 2*s.*

The Demonstration Frame, for Class Teaching,
on which the formation of almost any Stitch may be exhibited,
is used in the best German Schools. It may be had complete
with Special Needle and Cord. Price 5*s.* 6*d.*

Needlework, Schedule III., exemplified and Illustrated. By Mrs. E. A. CURTIS. Cloth.limp, with 30 illustrations, 1*s.*

"Needle Drill," "Position Drill," "Pin Drill," "Thimble Drill." Price 3d.

Drawing Book, Needlework Schedule III. Price 3*d.*

Directions for Knitting Jerseys and Vests, with scale for various sizes. By M. C. G. Especially suitable for elderly Ladies or Invalids. Dedicated by kind permission to Her Grace the Duchess of Marlborough. Sewed, 6*d.*

Crewel Work. Fifteen Designs in Bold and Conventional character, capable of being quickly and easily worked. With complete instructions. By ZETA, Author of "Ladies' Work, and How to Sell it," and including Patterns for Counterpanes, Bed Hangings, Curtains, Furniture Covers, Chimney-piece Borders, Piano Backs, Table Cloths, Table Covers, &c., &c. Demy, 2*s.* 6*d.*

Designs for Church Embroidery and Crewel Work from Old Examples. Eighteen Sheets, containing a Set of upwards of Sixty Patterns, with descriptive letterpress, collected and arranged by Miss E. S. HARTSHORNE. In a handsome cloth case, 5*s.*

MISCELLANEOUS BOOKS.

New Edition, enlarged.

The New Law of Bankruptcy. Containing the Bankruptcy Act, 1883, with Introduction, Tables, Notes, and an Index; to which is added a Supplement, containing the Orders, Forms, Fees, and List of Official Receivers. By ARCHIBALD BENCE JONES, M.A., Barrister-at-Law. Crown 8vo., cloth boards, price 5*s.*

Poker: How to Play it. A Sketch of the Great American Game, with its Laws and Rules. By one of its Victims. Cloth limp. Price One Shilling.

MISCELLANEOUS BOOKS—*(continued).*

"Great Paul," from its Casting to its Dedication. By S. J. MACKIE, C.E. With a Preface on Bells, by JOHN STAINER, M.A., Mus. Doc., Organist of St. Paul's. Illustrated. Price One Shilling.

Bicycles and Tricycles, Past and Present. A complete History of the Machines from their infancy to the present time, with Hints on How to Buy and How to Ride a Bicycle or a Tricycle, descriptions of the great Feats and Great Meets, &c., &c. By CHARLES SPENCER, Author of "The Bicycle Road Book," &c. Illustrated. 160 pp. Fcap 8vo, price One Shilling, or cloth, 1s. 6d.

The Cyclist's Road Book : compiled for the Use of Bicyclists and Pedestrians, being a Complete Guide to the Roads and Cross Roads of England, Scotland, and Wales, with a list of the best Hotels and notable places, &c., with map. By CHARLES SPENCER. Paper, 1s.; cloth, 1s. 6d.

The Confessions of a Médium. Crown 8vo., illustrated, price 3s. 6d.

Everyday Life in our Public Schools. Sketched by Head Scholars of Eton, Winchester, Westminster, Shrewsbury, Harrow, Rugby, Charterhouse. To which is added a brief notice of St. Paul's and Merchant Taylors' Schools, and Christ's Hospital. With a Glossary of some words in common use in those Schools. Edited by CHARLES EYRE PASCOE. With numerous Illustrations. Crown 8vo., cloth, new and cheaper edition, price 3s. 6d.

On Foot in France ; being a series of Papers contributed to the *Standard,* by FRANK IVES SCUDAMORE, Esq., C.B. Post 8vo., cloth, 2s.

A Complete GUIDE TO THE GAME OF CHESS, from the alphabet to the solution and construction of Problems. Containing also some Historical Notes. By H. F. L. MEYER, Chess Contributor to "The Boy's Own Paper," formerly Chess Editor of "Hannoversche Anzeigen," "The Gentleman's Journal," and "Eco Americano." Cloth, price 7s. 6d.

MISCELLANEOUS BOOKS—(*continued*).

Queen Mab; or, Gems from Shakespeare. Arranged
and Edited by C. W. A dainty bijou volume, uniform with The Churchman's Text Book, with illustrated title. Price 6*d.*

Maxims and Moral Reflections. By the Duc
DE LA ROCHEFOUCAULD. With his portrait, drawn by himself. A new translation by N. M. P. Diamond 48mo. Uniform with the above. Price Sixpence.

Caxton's Fifteen O's, and other Prayers.
Printed by command of the Princess Elizabeth, Queen of England and France, and also of the Princess Margaret, mother of our Sovereign Lord the King. By WM. CAXTON. Reproduced in Photo-lithography by S. AYLING. Quarto, bound in parchment. 6*s.*

WORKS FOR DISTRIBUTION.

A Woman's Secret; or, How to make Home
Happy. Thirty-third Thousand. 18mo., sewed, 6*d.*

By the same Author, uniform in size and price.

Woman's Work; or, How she can Help the Sick.
Nineteenth Thousand.

A Chapter of Accidents; or, the Mother's Assistant
in Cases of Burns, Scalds, Cuts, &c. Tenth Thousand.

Pay to-day, Trust to-morrow; illustrating the
Evils of the Tally System. Seventh Thousand.

Nursery Work; or, Hannah Baker's First Place.
Fifth Thousand.

The Cook and the Doctor; Cheap Recipes and
Useful Remedies. Sewed, 2*d.*

Home Difficulties. A Few Words on the Servant
Question. Sewed, 4*d.*

Family Prayers for Cottage Homes, with
Passages from the Scriptures. Sewed, 2*d.*

Taking Tales for Cottage Homes. Edited by

W. H. G. KINGSTON. 4 Vols., cr. 8vo., each containing three
Tales, cl. extra, 1*s.* 6*d.* each. 2 Vols., cr. 8vo., each containing
six Tales, cl. extra, bev. bds., 3*s.* 6*d.* each.

20 Vols., each containing separate Tale, price 6*d.* each.

1. **The Miller of Hillbrook**;
   a Rural Tale.
2. **Tom Trueman**, a Sailor in a
   Merchantman.
3. **Michael Hale and his
   Family in Canada.**
4. **John Armstrong, the Soldier.**
5. **Joseph Rudge,** the Australian
   Shepherd.
6. **Life Underground**; or, Dick,
   the Colliery Boy.
7. **Life on the Coast**; or, The
   Little Fisher Girl.
8. **Adventures of Two Orphans
   in London.**
9. **Early Days on Board a
   Man-of-War.**
10. **Walter the Foundling**; a
    Tale of Olden Times.
11. **The Tenants of Sunnyside
    Farm.**
12. **Holmwood**; or, The New
    Zealand Settler.
13. **A Bit of Fun and what it
    cost.** By A. LYSTER.
14. **Helpful Sam.** By Mrs. M.
    A. BARLOW.
15. **Sweethearts.** By Miss GER-
    TRUDE SELLON.
16. **A Wise Woman.** By F.
    BAYFORD HARRISON.
17. **Little Pretty.** By F. BAY-
    FORD HARRISON.
18. **Second Best.** By S. T.
    CROSS.
19. **Saturday Night.** By F.
    BAYFORD HARRISON.
20. **Little Betsey.** By Mrs. E.
    RELTON.

The Famous Women Library. By M. BETHAM

EDWARDS. 6 Vols., crown 8vo., cloth limp, price 6*d.* each.
Each Vol. contains a complete biography, with a steel plate
portrait, and about 40 pages of clear letterpress.

LIST OF BOOKS IN THE SERIES :—

I. **Fernan Caballero, Spanish Novelist.**
II. **Alexandrine Tinne, African Explorer.**
III. **Caroline Herschell, Astronomer and Mathematician.**
IV. **Marie Pape-Carpentier, Educational Reformer.**
V. **Elizabeth Carter, Greek Scholar.**
VI. **Matilda Betham, Littérateur and Artist.**

The "STANDARD AUTHORS" READERS,

ARRANGED AND ANNOTATED BY

THE EDITOR OF " POETRY FOR THE YOUNG."

THE Books have been planned throughout to meet exactly the requirements of the New Mundella Code. They are well printed from clear type, on good paper, bound in a strong and serviceable manner, and have *interesting and useful Illustrations from beginning to end.*

In the Infants' Books of the Series, very careful graduation in the introduction of sounds and words is combined with that great desideratum in Infants' Readers—an interesting *connected narrative form.*

The distinctive feature of the Series in the Higher Books is that the passages selected (both Prose and Poetry) are taken from the *Works of Standard Authors,* thus complying with the requirements of the New Code, and that they are of such a nature as to awaken, sustain, and cultivate the interest of youthful readers.

The Explanatory Matter is placed at the end of each Book, so that children may, at the discretion of the Teacher, be debarred access to it, and takes the form of three Appendices :—

> (*a*) **Explanatory Notes.**
> (*b*) **Biographical Notes.**
> (*c*) **A Glossary of Rare or Difficult Words.**

The compilation has been made with the utmost care, with the assistance and advice of gentlemen long conversant with the requirements of Public Elementary Schools ; and the Publishers feel that the literary, artistic, and mechanical excellences of the Books will be such that the Series will be pronounced

The "Ne Plus Ultra" of School Reading Books.

LIST OF THE BOOKS IN THE SERIES.

Primer, Part I., 16 pages, 18 Lessons, 14 Illustrations, paper ... 1d.
   ,,   ,, II., 48 ,, 43 ,, 31 ,, ,, ... 3d.
   ,,   ,, II A, being the first 32 pages of Primer II. ,, ... 2d.
Infant Reader, 64 pages, 55 Lessons, 32 Illustrations, cloth ... 4d.
   ,,   ,, (abridged) being the 1st 48 pp. of Infant Reader, cl. 3d.
   ,,   ,, (enlarged) ,, Infant Reader increased by 16 pages, cloth ... ... 5d.
Standard I. Reader, 96 pages, 51 Lessons, 29 Illustrations, cl. lp. 6d.
   Ditto ditto ditto ... ... cloth boards 8d.

,,	II.	,,	144	,,	61	,,	34	,,	... 9d.
,,	III.	,,	192	,,	62	,,	25	,,	... 1/-
,,	IV.	,,	288	,,	74	,,	26	,,	... 1/3
,,	V.	,,	320	,,	86	,,	22	,,	... 1/9
,,	VI.	,,	384	,,	92	,,	25	,,	... 2/-
,,	VII.	,,	384	,,	79	,,	26	,,	... 2/6

GRIFFITH & FARRAN,

WEST CORNER OF ST. PAUL'S CHURCHYARD, LONDON.